3D OF LIFE

3D OF LIFE

3D (Dimensions) of life
(Love, Support and Sacrifice)

PANKAJ GUPTA

ISBN:	Hardcover	978-1-4828-3915-9
	Softcover	978-1-4828-3914-2
	eBook	978-1-4828-3913-5

To order additional copies of this book, contact
Partridge India
000 800 10062 62
orders.india@partridgepublishing.com

www.partridgepublishing.com/india

He taught us to be Jovial in life.
He treated us as precious as Sapphire.
There was no Limit of his care for us.
His love to us was like Poetries to poet.
His touch to us was as soft as Lotus.
His Divine blessings are always with us.
His memories always Glitter in our heart.
I, as his Son always Energise with his memories.

Dedicated to my father, an architect of my life, my strength, inspiration and role model though he is no more but I always feel his presence around me.

Author's Note

"Life is a song - sing it.
Life is a game - play it.
Life is a challenge - meet it.
Life is a dream - realize it.
Life is a sacrifice - offer it.
Life is love - enjoy it."
Sai Baba

Whenever I read this quote, I always feel that life has many colours and that if we really want to live a meaningful life, then we must look at every colour and understand and appreciate its depth. The moment we understand this, life will open itself up for us in all its beauty, in all glory, and in all its splendour.

In this story, I have only played around with a few of the colours from the entire palette that constitutes life is really too big and too huge for anyone to deal with in entirety. I have tried, to the best of my abilities, to create as nuanced a story as possible, but there is a possibility that I might not have done full justice to the complexities of life. There is much that I too have to learn and experience in life and what gaps there are in the story, spring from this very fact.

But everything said and done, I do hope you enjoy the people and the world that I have created with my words. And do please share your comments once you finish the story, your insight and your feedback will go a long way in helping me improve my skill and my passion.

Thank You.

Chapter 1

When Sunil enters her office, he finds Shalini standing by the window of her second-floor office, staring at the slum on the other side of the road. He knows she is looking at a particular young boy, for she has often told him about him. She has observed the boy grow up on the street—crying for his mother, crawling through the dirt and filth, trying to walk, stumbling, falling, running, growing up, getting into fights with other slum boys, playing, and flying kites. So clearly lost is she in her reverie that Sunil knows she has neither heard him knocking on the door, nor is she aware of his having entered the room.

"Ahem," he clears his throat to catch Shalini's attention.

"Oh!" Shalini exclaims as she turns around and finds him standing in her office. "Sunil! Hi! How are you? I didn't even hear you come in . . ."

"I am good, Shalini. How are you?" Sunil smiles. The generally happy-to-go-lucky Shalini is clearly a little distracted today.

"I-I am all right . . ." she smiles and trails off, turning her attention back to the slum children flying kites across the road. The weather, she notes with a soft smile, is perfect for flying kites, the sky dark and heavy with the promise of rains and the wind a firm nudge to the kites, making them soar up and up and up.

"So Sunil," she asks after a moment, "what brings you to my office today?"

Shalini's question throws Sunil completely off balance. Doesn't she remember that this is their scheduled weekly review meeting?

"Shalini . . . ummm," Sunil hesitates, ". . . it's our weekly project status review meeting. But, umm . . . if you are busy, we can reschedule it for later . . ."

"No, no!" Shalini quickly dismisses his suggestion. "We will have our meeting right now." She walks back to her chair and gestures to him to take a seat as well.

Sunil nods and quickly sets up his laptop for the presentation. "Shalini, all our projects are going quite well except for one project, Lunar Eclipse Inc, where you and I need to talk to the client because he is suddenly unhappy with the overall progress of the project. Admitted, that we are running almost a month behind schedule, but he is aware that this delay is through no fault of ours, but you know how irrational and difficult clients can be. He is becoming a nuisance now, Shalini, with his constant complaints and—"

"Wait a minute Sunil!" Shalini cuts him short. "Delay? What delay are you talking about? I instructed you, very clearly and particularly, to take the best resources we have and complete this project on time. So where has this 'delay' come in from? What's going on Sunil? How can you let things slide like this?!"

Sunil can only stare at Shalini. Never before has he seen her react like this. Never before has he heard her talk like this, raise her voice like this. "Shalini, I-I . . ." he flounders, looking for words to explain his predicament. Shalini's stern face is not helping him either. "Shalini, thing is, ahem, we can easily absorb a couple of weeks of delay, but not an entire month's delay . . ."

"An entire month?!!! Sunil, this is unacceptable! To come to me for help at the very last minute! You should have apprised me of the situation earlier, much earlier. Why did you not say a word about any of this during our discussion last week?"

"Didn't want to bother you . . ." Sunil mumbles. "But Shalini," he looks up at her, pleading with her silently to understand, "I had kept the Lunar Eclipse program manager updated about the exact status of things and they knew about the delay and the reason behind it, and-and," Sunil falters a little before he continues, "and they were quite amenable to the change in plans until last week. That's why I didn't bring it to your notice. The client's manner led me to assume that they will approve the revised project plan, but suddenly, they've done a complete reversal, a full U-turn."

"Enough Sunil!" Shalini's voice is louder now, harsher too. "I do not want to listen to your excuses anymore. Go back and work out a plan to ensure we adhere to the timelines we have committed to. I cannot, I will not go and ask the client to make adjustments in their schedules because of your incompetence. And I want to see your plan in the next one hour. Is that understood?"

Sunil nods as he quickly shuts down his laptop and leaves Shalini's office. More than anything else, more than feeling angry or humiliated, he is confused about Shalini's strange behaviour. They've been working together for the past what, three or maybe four years, and something like what just happened, has never occurred before. He has never seen her losing her patience. Never. And definitely not like this. She is famous, in fact, for her ability to keep her cool even in the most trying of situations. And it isn't like this is the first time in the history of the company that a project is going to be slightly delayed. Projects get delayed few of the time and for critical projects, this number further increases due to complexity! Sunil shakes his head. She must have had a fight with her husband in the morning, he decides and sniggers. That would explain her irrational reaction. But then, he knows Shalini and Amit, her husband. They've all spent so much of time together, the families celebrating many festivals together and taking short holidays together. He knows for a fact that Shalini and Amit are not the kind of people who'd bring their domestic troubles to their workplace. And as for him and Shalini, they've always had a good working relationship and more than being his supervisor, she was the mentor everyone wished for. So what happened today? Why such an angry, volatile reaction?

The sudden ringing of his mobile phone interrupts his thoughts. Taking it out of his pocket, he is surprised to see its Shalini calling. What now? What does she want now? Hesitating, he picks the call.

"Sunil," Shalini says without waiting for even a hello, "are you on your seat?"

"No . . . just about to reach . . ."

"Okay, I am coming downstairs. Let's go for a coffee."

"Coffee?" Sunil is perplexed. First she shouts at him, and now she wants to have coffee? Was she going to dump some bad news on him? Hesitant and half-afraid, he manages a "Sure," before Shalini disconnects the phone. More than a little confused, he reaches his cubicle and has hardly managed to put his laptop down when Shalini is standing in front of him and gesturing to him to hurry up. She smiles a little stiffly when he looks up at her and he smiles back, not knowing what else to do than reciprocate.

Two minutes later, both of them are walking out of their office, the weather outside a welcome relief from the cloying atmosphere of their air-conditioned office. The Western disturbance has been gathering strength and the day's forecast warns of heavy downpour in the night.

"Let's walk down to Cafe Coffee Day, shall we?" Shalini asks.

"Sure thing," Sunil replies, knowing that Shalini likes to walk the short distance to Cafe Coffee Day, especially if the weather is good.

They walk silently all the way to Cafe Coffee Day—one, lost in her own thoughts, and the other fearing what lay ahead for him. Sunil is bursting with questions, but he dare not to ask any.

Cafe Coffee Day, as always, is quite crowded when they walk in a few minutes later. From students cribbing about classes and boring teachers to young couples making grand future plans, married couples talking over domestic issues, business men in crisp suits finalizing deals, girls discussing boys, and boys discussing girls, the café is always alive and vibrant with the hum of conversation. Shalini and Sunil find themselves a corner table for two and settle down. Sunil is beginning to feel increasingly uncomfortable with Shalini's silence. Finally, gathering some courage, he clears his throat and speaks up, "So, Shalini, what will you have? The usual cappuccino and sandwich? Or something else?"

"The usual is fine, Sunil, thanks . . ."

Sunil nods and gets up to go to the counter and place the order—two large cappuccinos and two cheese-and-tomato sandwiches. Since there is quite a rush, the boy at counter informs him, it will take at least twenty minutes to make their order ready.

"That's all right," Sunil says and walks away.

When he reaches their table, Sunil finds Shalini looking out of the huge glass window they are sitting next to. It's beautiful outside and Sunil knows that Shalini enjoys the outdoors, especially when Mumbai is on the brink of rain. Something about the rain and the sea, she had once told him. She smiles when he sits down.

"Sunil," she begins, "I must apologise to you for what happened earlier, in my office. Needless to say, I know you are a good worker. Why don't we review the whole situation again tomorrow? That should give you some time to come up with an alternative plan, right?"

Sunil is more than a little taken aback by Shalini's words. One minute she is screaming at him and now she is apologising? Saying he is a good worker? "Err . . . thank, Shalini, I, ahem, I appreciate that," he says.

Shalini only nods and turns her gaze back to the window.

"Shalini," Sunil speaks up a heartbeat later, his voice hesitant, "may I ask you a question?"

"Yes, of course . . ."

"Perhaps I should not be asking you any question, but, Shalini, you have always treated me more like a younger brother and less like a colleague . . ."

"Sunil, don't hesitate so much . . . just ask me what you want to."

"Shalini, I can see that something is bothering you. Why don't you tell me what it is? Perhaps I can help you figure out a solution?"

Shalini looks away from Sunil and is silent for a full minute before she replies to his question, "Thank you, Sunil, for extending your help. But it is only a small thing which, I am sure, will sort itself out in a couple of days."

"You know if you share your problems, you will only feel lighter . . ."

"Hmm . . ." Shalini goes back to observing the gathering clouds outside. "Sunil, look outside," she says. "The weather is really great today. If it stays like this till Friday, then we should plan a half-day team outing. What do you say?"

Sunil nods his head. He realises that she is trying to change the subject and divert his attention away from questioning her about whatever it is that is bothering her. "Shalini," he says gently, "I will take care of everything for this team outing, but before that, you need to tell me what's going on in your mind. What's troubling you Shalini?"

A waiter interrupts them with their order. As he places the steaming cups of cappuccinos in front of them, the smell of rich coffee makes both Sunil and Shalini smile appreciatively. They both love their coffees and are not very tolerant of the generally badly made cups of coffee that get passed around in their office. As soon as the waiter leaves, Sunil, tearing open a sachet of sauce and squeezing it out onto his plate, turns back to Shalini.

"Shalini, I am not going to leave you alone like this. I want to know what is bothering you."

"Sunil, please, trust me," Shalini pleads with him, "There is nothing bothering me!"

"I have known you long enough to know that you are lying, Shalini . . . and you know me, and I will not give up until you tell what the matter is."

"All right, Sunil," Shalini sighs, giving up. She knows she is fighting a losing battle against Sunil's determination to help her out. "I will tell you what's going on, but let's first have some coffee at least? You know how I always like to enjoy this kind of weather with a cup of hot coffee . . ."

When she smiles, Sunil nods his head and gestures to her to begin. They allow themselves to savour the warmth of their coffees and they wrap themselves in the noises of the cafe—people talking, orders being called out, coffee being made, a grinder running, a door opening and closing, cell phone ringing, and music playing softly in the background.

When she is halfway through her sandwich, Shalini picks up a sugar sachet and tearing it open, empties it into her coffee. She picks up stirrer and starts stirring the sugar slowly, a thoughtful expression on her face. "For about a week now," she speaks up suddenly, taking Sunil a little by surprise, "Amit has been quite disturbed. Obviously, I asked him many times about what's troubling him, but he is just not willing to share anything. Not only he is refusing to answer my questions, but also he seems to be withdrawing more and more into himself. He has also stopped going to work. All my endeavours in finding out what's wrong have been nothing but a waste."

Shalini takes a pause and then continues.

"The more I try to talk to him, the more Amit pulls away from me. Not knowing what else to do, I just left things as they were, but I know it's not the right thing to do. I am at my wits end now, Sunil, and I do not like to see my husband so troubled and so worried. I wish he'd say something, anything!"

Sunil has known Amit since the time Shalini got married to him. Amit writes scripts for television serials and quite a few of his serials are very famous and popular. Sunil knows for a fact that Amit is doing quite well for himself and that money is not a problem. Was it then that Amit's unfulfilled dream of being a mainline story writer was nagging him? Both Shalini and Amit actually belonged to Delhi, but Shalini had asked for a transfer to Mumbai in order to be with Amit as he pursued his dream. It has been five years since they first stepped into the city and Amit was still struggling to break away from the monotony of television and give concrete shape to his real ambitions.

"Shalini, have you tried talking to any of his friends? Perhaps they might know something?"

"Sunil, you know how these writers are . . . they don't really have many friends. Their lives are mostly restricted to the worlds they create on paper . . . apart from me, I don't think Amit really talks to anyone else about his feelings . . . and now he's stopped talking to me as well!"

"Hmm . . ." Sunil ponders over what Shalini has said. While what she said about writers being introverts is true, Amit has always been quite frank and open with him. He isn't typically broody and silent like a writer either. Sunil realises that something must be really upsetting Amit for him to behave like this.

"Well, Shalini," Sunil quips, wanting to lighten the atmosphere, "we need to solve Amit's problem as soon as possible as our office cannot afford to have stressed angel!"

Shalini smiles and shakes her head. She knows that all her colleagues call her an angel. The next moment, she bangs her hand on the table, excitement lighting up her eyes, causing Sunil to jump and look at her in surprise. "Sunil!" she exclaims, "I have an idea. Why don't you come home today evening for a little while and try talking to Amit? You know him very well. He might just open up to you!"

"Hmm . . . I guess I could try . . . I mean I am willing to do anything to help you guys out . . ." Sunil pauses for a second before continuing, "well, sure, let's do it . . . let's give this a shot."

"Great! So let's leave around six? We'll head straight to my house. Make sure you call home and tell them that you will be late."

"Yeah well, no real need to do that . . . I think all IT professionals' families know that there are no fixed timings for our work!" Sunil replies sarcastically.

Shalini stares at him but does not say anything.

Once done with their coffees, Sunil and Shalini walk out of Cafe Coffee Day and make their way back to office. For the rest of the afternoon, Sunil busies himself in finishing all his pending work so that he is free to leave with Shalini at six in the evening.

* * *

They leave together in the evening, Sunil driving behind Shalini all the way to Lokhandwala where she lives. Shalini's flat is on fourteenth floor and when they ring the doorbell to her house, Amit, who opens the door, is obviously surprised to see Sunil there.

"Sunil! Hey man! What a pleasant surprise!" Amit exclaims. "Shalini, you never told me Sunil is coming over!"

"Wanted it to be a surprise for you!" Shalini replies, grinning.

"Well, it is a surprise for me for sure. A great one, really. Please, come in, come in."

Amit steps aside and ushers Sunil and Shalini in and closes the door behind them.

The house is a nice, big three-bedroom flat. It's airy and very beautifully done-up, a proof of Shalini's excellent taste. Since he knows his way around the house, Sunil heads straight for the drawing-cum-dining room and makes himself comfortable on one of the brown leather sofas that Shalini has.

"So, Sunil, what will you drink?" Shalini asks, walking in behind Sunil.

"Why are you even asking him this question, Shalini? Don't we always have the same drink?" Amit interrupts, teasing his wife.

"No, no, Amit, not today," Sunil hurriedly replies. "Nothing but a Coke."

"What? A Coke? Are you sure?" Amit asks, looking a little surprised.

"Yes, I need to drive back . . ." Sunil walks up to the huge balcony and stares at the overcast sky outside. If it starts raining too heavily then he will have difficulty getting home. Mumbai roads during the rains were a danger to one and all.

Deciding to get Amit talking as soon as possible, Sunil walks back to his seat.

Shalini, meanwhile, has disappeared into the kitchen. Sunil can hear her instructing the maid to get the glasses and also bring some salted peanuts and some chips along with the Coke and the whisky.

The moment she re-enters the room half a minute later, the maid walking in behind her with a loaded tray in her hands, Amit looks up at her and grins. "Shalini," he says, "look at the weather outside . . . isn't it lovely? Just perfect for some spicy hot *pakoras* don't you think?"

Nodding her head, Shalini simply turns to the maid and tells her to start readying the batter for the *pakoras*. "You'll get your *pakoras* in fifteen minutes, Amit," she says as she serves them their drinks and passes the peanuts around. "Start with your drinks and I'll be back in a jiffy!" Shalini snaps her fingers and hurries back into the kitchen.

"So, how's work, Sunil?" Amit enquires as Shalini leaves the room.

"It is going great, just the same old stuff, really . . . nothing different, nothing new to be honest," Sunil replies, taking a sip of the Coke. "Our industry is very monotonous, you know. The same kind of projects, the same demanding deadlines, the same difficult clients," he continues, "but there is lot of excitement in your industry. All the new twists and turns you guys have to keep coming up with to keep your audience glued to the television. So you tell me what is going on at your end?"

Amit shifts in his chair. The cheerfulness that had been evident in his manner until a second ago now fades a little. Sunil notes that his face has become rather serious. Amit puts his glass of whisky back on table and picks up a handful of peanuts.

Picking one up, he stares at it for a long moment and, taking a deep breath, he says, "You know, Sunil, I think all industries looks exciting and intriguing from the other side. I mean, I think that your work is better than mine and here you are, thinking that mine is better than yours . . . you know the old saying? The grass is always greener on the other side?"

"Yes, of course, and it's true as well. We are always more interested in and attracted to what others have. But, Amit, our finding the grass greener on the other side can also make us feel motivated enough to work better, to improve ourselves, don't you think?"

"True . . . But it is not so easy, is it? This self-motivation that you are talking about?" Amit asks wryly.

This is the perfect opening to get to the bottom of the matter, Sunil thinks to himself. He looks at Amit and decides to go ahead with his question. "I might be wrong here," he begins a little hesitantly, "but I think there is more to what you just said than just a lack of self-motivation. Looks like you are not happy with your work, Amit . . ." Sunil hopes his question has not offended Amit. He doesn't want to appear unnecessarily nosy, but for Shalini's sake he has to at least try and get Amit talking.

"No, not Sunil . . . it's not that," Amit hurries to assure him. "I mean, it's not that I am unhappy with my work, but I am stuck in a phase, in a rut of sorts, where, if I don't pull myself through fast enough, I am in danger of staying stuck forever."

"I agree, Amit, but I also think that if one is caught in a stalemate, then one should not shy away from seeking help, especially from one's near and dear ones."

"You are right, but it also true that you will never turn to those closest to you for help unless you believe that it is your last resort and that there is nothing else that you can do, nowhere else that you can go to for assistance . . . nobody wants to deliberately upset their loved ones, right?" Amit reverts while taking another sip.

"I understand your dilemma, Amit, I do. I mean, if I were to be in some trouble, burdening my family with it would probably be the last thing I would ever do. I would always try to solve it myself. But, sometimes I think, one should share one's troubles . . ." Sunil smiles encouragingly at Amit. "Try telling me what's bothering you and perhaps you will feel a little lighter and that might just help you resolve your difficulty."

Shalini enters the room just then with a plate full of *pakoras*. The appetising smell of the *pakoras* makes Sunil's stomach grumble and he realises that he hasn't eaten anything since that early afternoon coffee with Shalini.

"When the weather is good, one is allowed to give in to one's mortal temptations," Amit grins as he picks up a piping hot *pakora* from the plate the minute Shalini puts it down on the table. "Oww!" he exclaims, juggling the *pakora* between his hands, "this is too hot, man!"

Shalini and Sunil laugh. "Of course it's hot Amit!" Shalini chides him. "I just took it off the gas." Then, turning to Sunil, she says, "Sunil, let's have dinner together, by the time you drive back home and get down to having dinner, it will be very late in the night. You might as well eat here with us and then leave . . ."

"Yes, yes, Sunil," Amit joins in, "stay for dinner. We won't take no for an answer, will we Shalini?"

And before Sunil can say anything, Shalini and Amit have already decided on a quick menu and Shalini goes back into the kitchen to get the dinner preparations underway.

"Well, so that's that!" Amit exclaims, looking at Sunil with a smile on his face. "You could not have ever refused Shalini's butter chicken, Sunil. I know you like it a little too much to say no to dinner!"

"You guys caught me there," Sunil grins back before resuming the earlier conversation, "So, Amit, back to where we were . . . why don't you share your problem with me?"

"It's not that big a problem, Sunil, honestly."

"Come on, Amit," Sunil persists. "You know you can trust me with whatever is bothering you . . ."

"I know, I know . . ." Amit shrugs his shoulders a little helplessly. "It's just that . . . umm . . . I don't know . . ." he trails off, staring into the amber-coloured whisky in his glass.

"Try . . . try talking about it," Sunil suggests gently.

Finishing the rest of his drink in one gulp, Amit runs his hand through his hair. "It's just that, I am standing at peculiar crossroad in my career. If I manage to choose the correct direction, I know I will be so successful that only the sky will be the limit. But if I don't manage to do what is required of me, then I will remain where I am, stuck in a rut . . . living the same life day in and day out for every day of the rest of my life."

"Hmm . . ."

"You know how long I have been working in this industry, but I am mostly still where I started. Climbing up the ladder in the entertainment industry is really tough, but I am afraid that my progress has been especially slow. Five years in Mumbai, Sunil, in this city of dreams, and I am still not a lead storywriter!

It is frustrating, yes, but I didn't ever lose faith in myself, in my skill as a writer. I thought I was unable to achieve my dream because there were no opportunities around. But guess what, Sunil? I have the opportunity now, but my ability to write has fled me. It's gone! Disappeared! Poof! Nothing left!"

"What do you mean, it's disappeared? And what opportunity are you talking about?" Sunil asks. When Amit simply shakes his head and again starts staring into his now empty glass, Sunil gets up and says, "Hey, give me your glass, let me make another drink for you, all right?"

Amit nods listlessly. He appears to be lost in his own thoughts. Sunil walks up to the mini bar in the dining room and pours Amit a drink. He knows he needs to be patient with Amit. The man is clearly on the brink of telling him what is going on, but too many questions and he might just shut up for good. Quickly making his way back to the drawing room, he hands Amit his drink and gestures to him to go.

"Well," Amit takes a quick sip of his drink and begins, "we recently got a half an hour prime-time slot at a top TV channel and Dwita, my boss, asked me to work out some interesting plotlines to pitch. Now, Dwita is like the superwoman of the television industry. She fought her way up with hard work and dedication and she's unbelievably good at what she does. It's been a dream comes true to work for her. She is inspiring . . . but she also sets very high standards though she is famous to pull it as long as the viewers demand it."

He takes a pause and then continues . . .

"For this prime-time slot, she wants me to work out a story which has a strong small-town flavour and which works around the ideas of love, responsibility, family, and personal sacrifice. Prime time means I have to come up with something really solid and really really interesting. Something different from the stuff already on TV, but at the same time, it should appeal to the people so that it can pick up the slot and lead in TRP. They should want to come back to the story every day. The characters should be real . . . I tried working out one too many plots in last one week, but not a single one is clicking."

Amit takes a deep breath and continues . . .

"I am simply unable to get that one 'just right' plotline. And if I do not present Dwita with something concrete in the next couple of days, she will either lose the slot in entirety or she will simply move on to some other writer which will essentially mean the death of my career. I do not want to miss this opportunity, Sunil, I do not. But, I am getting more and more nervous with each passing day and I have run out of ideas!" Amit falls silent.

Sunil has stiffened at Amit's words. When he does not say anything and remains silent, Amit looks up at him and immediately notices his strained and slightly distressed demeanour.

"Sunil? Are you all right?" Amit asks with concern.

"Yes, yes," Sunil mumbles, "I am quite all right . . . I, ahem," he clears his throat, "would you mind if I pour myself a drink?"

"Go right ahead, man," Amit says, curious as to what could have possibly upset Sunil to this extent that he wanted to pour himself a drink. Had he said something wrong? But he had only been talking about his work problems. Then what could the matter be?

When Sunil walks in a minute later with a drink in his hand, Amit looks at him questioningly. "Did I say something to upset you, Sunil?"

"No, not at all . . . on the contrary, your words brought back some memories," Sunil assures him, his voice so low that Amit has to lean forward to catch the words.

"What memories, Sunil? Why do I get this strange feeling that there is a story behind your words? A story we know nothing about?"

For the longest time, Sunil does not say anything. His face, Amit sees, is a mirror that reflects his emotions. There is pain, there is heartbreak, there is anguish, and there is suffering. What is Sunil's story? Amit wonders.

"It's a long story Amit," Sunil speaks up finally, "and one that is very difficult for me to share . . ."

"You can trust me with your story, Sunil. I might be a writer, but rest assured that I will not share a single word of your story with anyone unless you allow me to do so."

"It needs time . . ." Sunil says weakly.

"We have all the time in the world, my friend. The entire night stretches out ahead of us. Listen," Amit walks up to Sunil and puts a hand on his shoulder, "why don't you finish your drink while I go tell Shalini to make the guest room ready for you. You can stay here tonight. I'll tell her to eat and go to bed and not wait up for us. We'll eat when we want to, and you can call your home and tell your wife that you will be staying with us tonight. That's all right with you, buddy?"

Sunil only nods in response.

When Amit returns to the drawing room, he finds Sunil standing near the balcony, lost in is thoughts and memories. "Sunil?" he says.

"Oh!" Sunil turns around, taken a little unaware by Amit's return. "You're back already."

"Yeah. Got everything settled. Shalini will have dinner shortly and go to bed. She says that she's too tired to stay up with us. So, my dear old friend, we have the entire night for your story . . . Cheers, buddy!"

"Cheers!" Sunil says, smiling a little.

It has started to rain a little outside, and with each passing hour, Sunil knows it will only increase in intensity. It's good that he does not have to drive back home in the rain. He knows Amit is waiting for him to start with his story, but where to start? What words to use? How much to tell and how much to keep hidden away in the deepest corners of his mind? Or perhaps he should let all his fears and questions go. Perhaps he should let his heart talk and not his mind . . . and taking a deep, steadying breath, he begins.

* * *

Chapter 2

"I belong to the small town of Kalpi in Uttar Pradesh. It's right on the banks of the Yamuna. Perhaps you might have heard of Kalpi? It was one of the worst affected towns when Phoolan Devi and her gang of dacoits were at their peak. Anyhow, Kalpi is like any other typical small town. Everyone knows everyone else and it's like one, big family. Every marriage, every birth, every personal achievement, and every festival is a cause for celebration for the entire town. People stand by each other in good times and bad, mourning deaths and losses together. The town has many temples of interest and that lends a distinctly spiritual air to the place. Life starts really early in the morning in Kalpi with the ringing of the temple bells ushering in the new day and calling all worshippers to come pray. I remember my mother being freshly showered and ready with her small basket of flowers and her *puja thali* by five-thirty in the morning. The daily activities in our house would start only after her return from the temple about half an hour later. Mornings also meant a steady trickle of people going to the Yamuna to take a holy dip in the river before starting their day. And all of this came to a full circle with the evening *aarti* which signalled the end of the day and left people free to mingle and talk. Men would gather around small tea shops and discuss business and politics while the women swapped stories about domestic issues and friends and children. "My house was in the heart of the town and I lived with my parents and my younger sister. My father was a very well-respected cloth merchant and we had a decent-sized shop in the main market. I bet you won't be able to imagine just how chaotic and congested Kalpi's main market was. It was nothing like all these sprawling, air-conditioned malls that we have today. It was a long narrow road with shops squeezed one against the other along both sides. There would be a constant stream of people walking up and down through the market, navigating their way through the cycles, the scooters, the auto-rickshaws, and the stray cows crowding the road.

"Anyway, to tell you a little more about my family, my father is a very simple man who mostly keeps to himself. He had a fixed daily routine back then—get up early in the morning, have tea, bathe, pray, go to the shop, spend the day working there, come back at sundown, have tea, watch television, eat dinner, spend some time with us, and then sleep. I don't think I ever remember my father in anything but a *dhoti and kurta*. He is really a man of the soil, true to his roots. But I never really got to know my father as a person. Children back in those days were not so close to their parents. There was also that barrier of expected respect and deference between us.

"My mother has always been a deeply religious person. She used to be on some fast or the other for almost half the year. I am praying, she would say seriously, for the wellbeing of our family. She's stopped now, of course, age catches up with the body after all, doesn't it? But she still takes her bath only with cold water, even in the peak of winter. Can you imagine that? That old, frail-looking woman, getting up every day at the crack of dawn and taking a cold shower? I shiver just thinking about it. She is a good cook, my mother, and many an afternoon I spent stuffing myself on her *roti* and *daal*. She was quite strict, but we knew how to extract favours and work around her. We were the centre of her universe and she spent all her waking and sleeping hours worrying about our health and our well-being.

"My younger sister Sharda, is three years younger to me and when we were growing up, she would follow me just about everywhere I went. She would stick herself to me like a shadow. She was typical younger child, a little shy, a little naughty, a little irresponsible, and my father's favourite. She was my partner-in-crime until I outgrew her girlish ideas. I remember, whenever she wanted something and my parents refused her, she would come running to me and blackmail me into giving her my pocket money so that she could buy that doll she wanted, or that skipping rope she'd seen in the market, herself. She was, needless to say, a regular little monkey.

"As for myself, I was mostly an introvert. I didn't have many friends. Being the youngest amongst all the boys in the neighbourhood, I was, unfortunately, the butt of all their jokes and pranks. They never let go of an opportunity to humiliate me and make me feel miserable. They called me names, they refused to let me play with them, they teased me mercilessly about being a zero, in short, and they were just plain mean to me. I think that's what ended up making me so studious. I turned to books when they spurned my continuous efforts to befriend them.

"And thus, hours spent inside home, hiding from the mean neighbourhood boys, and keeping my nose glued to my books, became days, days became weeks, weeks became months, and months became my way of life. I had turned into a bookworm.

"Nothing spectacular, nothing exciting happened in my life. I went to school, I came back, ate lunch, slept a little, and spent the rest of the day studying and doing my homework. It was boring mostly. But there is this one incident which stands out in my memory. I know you will not believe what I am about to tell you, but let me go ahead with the story anyway . . .

"I was about eleven or maybe twelve at that time, I am not very sure. It was the month of March, the air getting heavier and hotter with every passing day, hinting at the approaching summer, even as spring blossomed in our gardens and lifted our spirits. My neighbour's son was getting married and almost the entire neighbourhood had been invited to travel with the groom as his *baraat* party. We were all to go to Jalaun, a town almost fifty kilometres away, for that's where the bride lived. My mother had made innumerable trips to the market to make preparations for the wedding, buying new clothes and new shoes for all of us. It was perhaps the first time I was going to be a part of an out-of-town wedding, and my excitement knew no bounds. I could hardly wait for the wedding day to come.

"When the day finally dawned, crisp, clear, and bright, I was out of my bed with a leap. My mother was surprised to see me up and about without her having to wake me up as was the usual case, but she smiled knowingly and handed me my cup of morning tea. The groom's house, about two doors away, had been abuzz with activity and celebrations for a good week now. Relatives and friends had been pouring into their house continuously and a general sense of great festivity had gripped the entire neighbourhood. From the kitchen window, I could see the *baraat* bus parked right behind my house. We were to leave a little after lunch. I remember the entire day passing by in a blur. My mother served us a quick simple lunch and hurried off to pack our new clothes into the small suitcase I was taking along. Father even gave me a hundred rupees note to keep with myself in case there was some kind of an emergency and I needed money. While I was mostly excited about going to Jalaun, I was also a little afraid of how the other neighbourhood boys would treat me. I would be exposed to their cruel taunts and jokes for the entire duration of the trip. But I decided to keep to myself and ignore them the best I could.

"The bus ride to Jalaun was fun. We were a group of about twenty-five to thirty people and everyone was in high spirits, singing, cracking jokes, chattering, and laughing the entire way. When we reached Jalaun in the early evening, we were greeted very graciously by the bride's family. They had booked one of the most famous guesthouses of their town for us and they directly escorted us there for refreshments.

"The hot *chai* and the tasty assortment of snacks revived us all sufficiently, and once done, we all retired to our rooms to get ready, for the *baraat* was scheduled to leave in a short while. The groom's father had hired a very famous band from Orai, a traditional and must part of any north Indian marriage, another town near Kalpi, and we could all hear the band party tuning their instruments in the courtyard outside and getting ready for the night ahead. The excitement and the energy inside the guesthouse was maddening. While the men and the boys got ready in less than five minutes, the women, very typically, took their own sweet time to get ready, decking themselves up in heavy silk saris and beautiful gold jewellery.

"And then, we were all finally ready to dance our way to the bride's house. The band started the *baraat* by playing that famous Hindi song '*Aaj mere yaar ki shadi hai*', you know, the one you hear in every Indian wedding? Well, so good were the band people in whipping up energy and enthusiasm that very soon, there was not one of us who was not dancing to their tunes and having fun. We all lost ourselves to the music and danced to our heart's content.

"When we finally reached the bride's house, we were greeted formally by her parents with a *puja thali* and a showering of flower petals. They were very nice people and they made us all feel very welcome.

"Since the bride's house itself was located at the end of a rather narrow lane, the actual arrangements for the wedding and for the marriage reception had been made in the open ground behind her house. It was a fairly huge ground with nothing but a big *pipal* tree in one corner near small pond.

"The entire ground, including the tree, had been decorated beautifully with marigold flowers and lights. We were all very impressed with the arrangements the bride's family had made. The stage that had been set up for the bride and the groom had been done up exceptionally nicely in white and yellow roses.

"While the men and the women in our *baraat* party went and sat on the chairs that had been lined up near the stage, all the children ran up to the *pipal* tree and sat on the wide circular platform running all around it. All this while, amidst all the celebration and all the dancing and laughing, I had been keeping my distance from the boys in the group. They had started to tease me a little when we had all been having tea and refreshments back at the guesthouse, but on seeing me ignore them, they had left me alone after a while. But now, with no adults around to stop them or scold them, the boys were beginning to get loud and rowdy. It was becoming increasingly difficult to ignore them and I was almost about to get up and go sit with my father when, much to my horror, I suddenly realised that the hundred rupee note which my father had given me earlier in the morning and which I had carefully into my pant pocket was now missing. Obviously a hundred rupee note in those days meant a lot, and I was naturally scared beyond belief. I could not very well go up to my father and tell him I had lost the money for he was sure to scold me for being irresponsible. Getting up abruptly, I retraced my steps all over the ground, looking under chairs and behind tables for my lost hundred rupee note. But I just couldn't find it. Dejected, I went back to the *pipal* tree and sat a little way off from the rest of the boys.

"The rest of the wedding passed in a daze. Apart from being already tired with the boys constantly teasing me, I was now extremely afraid of telling my father about what had happened. I couldn't concentrate on anything that was happening around me. The bride came out and went up to sit with the groom on the stage, they exchanged garlands, people clapped and hooted, the wedding rituals began and ended, but I literally saw nothing and heard nothing. Even dinner, tasty and excellent as I am sure it must have been, tasted like ash in my mouth.

"It was in the wee hours of the morning that we all came back to the guesthouse. Not bothering with anything or anyone else, I simply crashed into the bed that had been allotted to me.

"It was the next morning when the trouble started. I woke up with a blinding headache and a really bad stomach ache. One of our neighbours was a doctor and he quickly gave me some medicine, assuring my father that it was nothing but a case of indigestion and overeating perhaps. But even an hour after having taken the medicine, I felt no better than before. When we finally reached Kalpi late in the afternoon, I went straight to my room and lay down on my bed. I had not said anything to my parents about feeling increasingly worse, but when my mother came in later in the evening with a cup of tea in her hand, she found me shivering and my body burning with what appeared to be a raging fever. She ran and called my father and he immediately got a thermometer to check my temperature. It was hundred and two. Concerned, my mother asked my father to summon a doctor. My father nodded, looking just as worried as my mother.

"All this while, I had been restlessly tossing and turning on my bed. My legs had also started twisting inwards at an odd angle on their own account and my eyes seemed to have somehow focussed themselves on the ceiling and staring. Just as my father was about to leave the room, I spoke up, 'A doctor can't do anything now.'

"Both my parents jumped back in surprise for my voice had changed. It was heavier and older, not the voice of a twelve-year-old boy.

"'Wh-why-why?' my mother asked, sounding more than a little afraid.

"I turned to look at her and she yelped. My eyes were blank and my face had contorted itself uglily. 'This boy is unable to sustain me.'

"Now my mother understood what was happening. A spirit had taken possession of me! Gathering her wits about her, she immediately controlled herself and asked, 'Who are you?'

"When I just smiled and stared back at the ceiling, she asked again, 'Who are you?'

"'Ram Lal Verma.'

"'Where are you from? And why are you here, in my son's body?' she persisted.

"'I am from Jalaun, and I want to take this boy with me back to Jalaun to kill my murderers.'

"'But why this boy?' she asked again.

"'Because I liked him, that's why!'

"Without another word, my mother got up and left the room, signalling to my father to accompany her. Knowing that the immediate solution was to make me drink holy water, she hurriedly fetched some from the small altar we had at home. But, when she came back to my room and tried to make me drink it, I refused to take it. My resistance was so high that my father could not control me. My father immediately went out and got a couple of people to come take hold of me. And then, after lot of resistance, I was made to forcibly drink the holy water.

"I quieted down after that and eventually drifted off to sleep. But things were not over, not just yet.

"Come morning, and I was again running a high temperature. My father arranged for some priests to come over and do some special *puja* for me. That entire day, my house rang with the sound of mantras being chanted and prayers being offered. The smell of incense and sandalwood filled the entire house and when it drifted up to my room, all of it only made me more agitated. Nails were put all around my house on the priests' instructions to keep evil spirits at bay.

"It took three days for me to regain control of myself, and even after my body had been rid of the spirit, there were times when I used to see that someone was calling me from outside, but obviously there was no one around anywhere. I used to tell my mother and she suggested me not to look outside and ignore him for few days. For the first few days after all of this, I was not allowed to go out of the house at all. My soul, the priests had told my parents, had become very weak and was very susceptible to more such attacks. As I became stronger, I was allowed, at first, only to step out of the security of my home during daytime, and then, finally, after many many days, in the evenings as well.

"My mother, meanwhile, had asked me some questions about everything that had happened to me during the wedding in Jalaun. She had also made inquiries with the newly-married bride about a Ram Lal Verma and she had been told that there had indeed been a person with that name in Jalaun, but he had been murdered quite a while back and his body had been discovered hanging from the same *pipal* tree under which I had sat with the other boys . . ."

Sunil stops his story here. He knows Amit will have great difficulty in believing even a word of what he has just shared. When he looks at Amit, Amit just shakes his head with incredulity.

"Sunil," Amit begins after a moment, "what rubbish is this? Do you really expect me to believe all of this? Or perhaps you are just plain drunk already . . ."

"I do not really expect you to believe me, Amit," Sunil replies with a knowing smile, "but what I told you is true, every word of it. You can choose to not accept it, but that does not make it a lie because I went through it myself and it's not some hand-me-down story that I am narrating to you . . . I cannot discount what happened because that incident went a long way in making me focus my attention on strengthening my mind and my soul instead of letting myself be troubled with petty things like being made fun of by a bunch of stupid *mohalla* boys."

"Hmm . . . tell me Sunil, do spirits and ghosts and all these things exist only in villages and small towns? I mean, I am sorry, I guess, if I am sceptical, but you are the first person who is telling me that he has personally had such a close encounter with a spirit."

"I understand completely . . . sometimes, even I have difficulty believing that it really happened. But to answer your question, I am not sure if this is something which happens only in small towns and villages, but I think that perhaps wherever you find believers and people who are open to the existence of such alternate realities and being, these things exist there . . ."

"Quite possible. Anyway, give me your glass. It is empty."

Sunil gives his glass to Amit and sinks back into his chair as Amit goes to the mini bar to make a drink. Memories from his childhood days in Kalpi are flooding his mind now.

"Hey Sunil," Amit calls out, breaking Sunil's reverie. "It's past ten, man. Let's have dinner quickly and we can continue with your story then, huh?"

"Sure thing," Sunil says, nodding his head. He walks over to join Amit in the dining room and both of them quickly get down to eating the butter chicken and the *rotis* that Shalini has made for them.

"Good food, huh?" Amit asks after the first bite.

Sunil nods his head in agreement. Shalini has always been a great cook and he has always liked coming to her house for dinners and lunches. Even his wife is in love with Shalini's butter chicken. Pity, she is missing the dinner.

They finish the rest of the meal in complete silence, too busy savouring the food to bother talking. When they are done, they refresh their glasses of whisky at the bar and walk back to the drawing room where Amit, after settling himself comfortably on one of the sofas and stretching his legs out in front of him, gestures to Sunil to continue with the story. Sunil, taking a quick small sip of his whisky, picks up the thread of his story from where he had left it of before dinner.

Chapter 3

"August 18th, 1998. I still remember date, for that was when the steady rhythm of my days got disrupted and the course of my life changed irrevocably.

"Years had passed between the Jalaun incident I just told you about and this seemingly normal day in August. I was about seventeen and I was sitting in my classroom at school, and our Hindi teacher, Yadav Sir, was explaining the meaning of a poem to us. He was a very popular man, Yadav sir, and unlike in other schools where Hindi was almost always the most boring subject of all, in our school, we all waited eagerly for Yadav sir's class. He always tried to be more of a friend to us than a strict teacher and he spoke to us with such openness that we could not help but like him immensely. Anyhow, Yadav sir was in the middle of explaining to us boys the meaning of the word '*kanchuki*' which was part of one the couplets of famous poet Soordasji.

"'Do any of you know the meaning of the word *kanchuki*?' he asked.

"Now, we all knew that his explaining the meaning of the word was one of his favourite moments in class since our seniors had already told us about it. Therefore, when he asked us the question, all of us shook our heads and shouted, 'No Sir!'

"'No matter, no matter,' Yadav sir assured us, 'Let me explain it to you . . .'

"Some of the boys sniggered in the back rows as Yadav sir got up from his chair and came to stand in front of his table. 'Do you know,' he asked very seriously, 'what women wear?'

"'*Sari*!' all the students shouted in unison.

"'Yes, of course. But what else so they wear?'

"When none answered, he looked around the class encouragingly. 'Come on now, don't be shy. Anyone wants to try?'

"Someone timidly said, 'Sir, blouse.' Yadav sir nodded in agreement and then, smiling at us conspiratorially, he said, 'Women wear blouses, yes, and what they wear underneath a blouse is the *kanchuki*. So, you boys have learnt a new word today, huh?' He laughed a little and then in mock seriousness he continued, 'But don't you guys forget the actual poem we were discussing, okay? Knowing the meaning of *kanchuki* won't help you pass the exam!" We were all laughing at sir's little joke when suddenly; someone interrupted the class from outside.

"'Excuse me, sir? May I come in?'

"A girl. About five-foot two, very fair, pretty eyes, shoulder length hair tied neatly in a ponytail, carrying two notebooks in her hand, and not dressed in the school uniform. All of us were looking at her curiously and it was easy to see that under the scrutiny of so many pairs of eyes, the girl was beginning to feel a little uncomfortable.

"Yadav sir beckoned her in. 'Come in, come in. What do you want?'

"'Sir,' the girl came in, 'my name is Madhu Trivedi, and I have taken admission in this class . . .'"

"Wait a minute!" Amit exclaims, breaking into Sunil's story. "Madhu? Madhu Trivedi?!"

"Yes yes, I know what you are going to say, Amit, but let me finish the story first. You can put two and two together later on, okay?" Sunil laughs and waves him off, knowing very well what question Amit is about to ask. But he does not want to rush into the future and tell Amit about what happens. He is reliving his past as he is narrating the story and he does not want to jumble the string of events up. Amit grumbles a little but gives in and gestures to Sunil to continue with the story.

"So yes," Sunil picks up the story again, "I was telling you that the new girl interrupts the class and tells Yadav sir her name.

"'In this class?' Yadav sir exclaimed a little incredulously. 'And that too in the middle of the session?'

"'Yes sir, actually my father works with the PWD and he has just been transferred to Kalpi. That's why I am joining the school mid-session,' the girl explained.

"'But why this section? Did nobody tell you that we have a separate girls' section?' Yadav sir enquired.

"'Yes sir however I have mathematics as a main subject and the girls section has biology instead of maths, therefore, I was asked to join this section.'

"'Hmm . . . all right then,' Yadav sir nodded his head.

"'Sunil,' he called out, 'you will help Madhu get to know the entire class and you will also assist her in catching up with as much of the course as has been covered in this session. Is that understood?'

"'Yes sir,' I replied. I was extremely aware of the fact that all the other boys in the class were staring at me. I knew what they were all thinking, that I was extremely lucky to have been appointed the official helper to the new girl standing in front of us. I stole a quick look at her and realised, in one bright split second that is still etched clearly in my heart, that she was the most beautiful girl I had ever seen.

"The bell rang for recess just then and smiling genially at everyone, Yadav sir gathered his books from the teacher's table and walked out of the classroom.

"I walked up to the new girl, a little shy, a little eager, and a little afraid I'd say something stupid and make a fool of myself. 'Hi, I am Sunil,' I said, managing not to fumble, and extended my hand to her.

"Smiling, she shook my hand and said, 'Hi, I am Madhu.'

"Over the next forty-five minutes, while the entire school busied itself in enjoying the mid-day recess, playing football, walking around the sports field, talking, laughing, chattering, running around, and eating, I sat in a quiet corner with Madhu and chatted with her. She told me briefly about her family and I told her about mine and also brought her up to date with what all had already been covered in the term's syllabus. How the minutes flew away, I still don't know, but the next thing I knew, the bell was ringing, recess was over, and we were walking back to the classroom.

"And that was when, I believe, my heart first starting beating for someone else . . ."

CHAPTER 4

"So you fell in love!" Amit exclaimed, a broad smile on his face.

"Yeah well . . . maybe . . ." Sunil replied thoughtfully. "But at that point in time, I was not even aware of what it is like to fall in love with someone. All I knew was that something somewhere felt different and that I wanted to know as much about Madhu as was possible."

"Well go on go on with what happened next, I am all ears to hear about this young Sunil," Amit urged.

"Hmmm . . . so," Sunil began, going back to the August of his first love. "It was on the night of *Janmashtami* that I got a chance to talk to Madhu outside of school. Until now, all our interactions had been limited to me helping her out with schoolwork in between classes.

"*Janmashtami* is a very popular festival in Kalpi in fact in entire North India, and all the Lord Krishna's temples around the town would set up volunteer committees, months in advance, to oversee the celebration of the festival. I was also helping out in the volunteer committee in the temple closest to my home. In fact, all the boys from my neighbourhood were there as well. We had been busy since morning decorating the temple premises with garlands and lights. While most of us were engaged in readying the temple for the festivities in the evening, four of the boys went to the main market to get food packets for our lunch. When they came back about an hour or so later, they were all laughing and sniggering and generally making fun of a boy named Karan who had gone to the market with them. I wondered, naturally, about what must have happened in the market to make them ridicule Karan, but with so much left to do and take care of, there was hardly any time to bother with such a petty issue.

"We finished all the work only by six in the evening. The first of the devotees were expected to come in by about nine in the night, which gave us roughly an hour to go home, freshen up, get ready, and report back to the temple for our duties.

"I went home, showered, changed quickly into a blue kurta and a white pyjama, and was back at the temple by a quarter to seven. I was assigned the duty of managing the movement of devotees at the temple gate to make sure that there was a controlled coming and going of people and that the crowd does not get unruly. My partner in this was Karan.

"As expected, by nine the devotees started coming in. It started as a trickle, but within the next forty-five minutes, the entire temple hall was full. As more and more people started queuing up outside, the crowd began spilling out of the main temple hall into the temple grounds. *Janmashtami* festival was in full swing now.

"It was such a mad sea of people inside the temple and outside, that I could not help but feel a little lost in that sea of faces. And suddenly, right in the middle of that confusing sea of faces, I saw her, Madhu, standing in line with her family to get into the temple. I stared at her, realising, once again, just how beautiful she was, especially dressed as she was in a lovely light yellow *salwar kameez*. She caught my eye and I couldn't help breaking into a smile. She smiled back, her smile warm and beautiful, and my heart started beating just a little faster. And then, in the blink of an eye, the line crept up enough for her to be standing right in front of me at the gate.

"'Hi Sunil,' she greeted me.

"'Hi Madhu, nice to see you here,' I replied a little shyly.

"'Meet my parents and my younger brother,' she said, introducing me to her family.

"'*Namaste* Uncle, *Namaste* Aunty,' I greeted her parents respectfully.

"'*Namaste beta*,' her father replied with a smile. 'Looks like there is no space inside . . . quite a rush, huh?' he commented. Then, turning to his wife, he told her to sit outside the temple and enjoy the *bhajans* being sung inside while they waited for the rush inside to lessen a little bit.

"I didn't want Madhu and her parents to wait outside the temple like that. And though there was indeed a full crowd inside, I insisted that space could always be made for four more devotees. 'I'll take you all inside, Uncle,' I offered, thinking that I could help them make their way through the throng of people inside and that Karan could handle the situation at the gate on his own for a couple of minutes. But, when I turned around to tell him of my decision, Karan was nowhere to be seen! He had simply disappeared! Perplexed, I made a split-second decision to abandon my post at the gate and entrust it to another member of the volunteer committee while I escorted Madhu and her family inside.

"We had to literally push our way past the people inside, but most of them were lost to the spell cast by the *bhajans* being sung and nobody really minded. I found some space in the temple hall for Madhu's mother and father to sit in, but it wasn't enough to seat all four of them. Therefore, I brought Madhu and her brother Ravi out to the garden and we started taking a slow walk around it.

"'So, Ravi, which class do you study in?' I asked after some time to break the silence.

"'Class five,' the boy replied.

"'Good good. And which school have you taken admission in?'

"'I haven't taken admission yet. *Papa* said that we will do it next week.'

"'I see . . .' I desperately wanted to talk to Madhu, but with her brother around, I knew I had to first have a polite round of conversation with him. Also, Madhu was walking a step behind us as she was busy admiring the lovely flowers the temple garden boasted of. She didn't seem really interested in making small talk.

"'What are your hobbies, Ravi?' I asked, hoping Madhu would join in and stop looking at the flowers.

"'I love to play with sand and make sandcastles!' Ravi exclaimed happily.

"'Wow! What a coincidence! I love making sandcastles as well!'

"Ravi grinned and skipped ahead, leaving me alone to wait for Madhu to catch up.

"'Ravi!' she called out after her brother when she saw him running ahead. 'Don't wander away or *Mummy Papa* will scold you,' she warned him.

"'I won't, *Didi!*' Ravi called back.

"And finally, I was alone with Madhu. She smiled when she came up to me.

"'So, what were you two talking about?' she asked.

"'Just this and that . . . I was asking Ravi about his hobbies,' I replied.

"'Hmm . . .'

"'So, what about you? What are your hobbies, Madhu?' I asked, wanting to know more and more about her. I wanted to walk like this with her for as long as I could.

"'Well, I love reading,' she said with a smile, 'particularly history. I am really passionate about it. And when I read about something which happened a long long time back, there are times when I actually feel like I have been somehow transported back to that era and the story is really unfolding slowly all around me . . . it's really amazing, you know . . .'

"She spoke at length about her passion for history and how she could spend hours and hours lost in stories about ancient worlds. And all the while, I could only stare at her and marvel at the depth of her passion. We had found ourselves a spot on the lawn to sit on, and as she talked, I just watched her face. Her beauty, her innocence, and her purity enchanted me and, when the temple conch shells blew at midnight signalling the birth of Lord Krishna, I was all but lost in her.

Chapter 5

"The day after *Janmashtami* being a Sunday, I was in no hurry to get up early and by the time I actually got out of bed it was around ten. I know my sister had walked in a couple of times to wake me up, but after all the magic of the previous night, I was too caught up in my dreams to hear her calls.

"I was having breakfast when I heard someone shouting my name from outside. It was Akash, one of the boys from the neighbourhood. In fact, he was the leader of that entire pack of bullies I detested. I got up and went outside and saw that apart from Akash, there were five more boys with him—Sharad, Vikas, Santosh, Manoj, and even Karan. I was quite surprised. Never before had they ever come to my house. And they were all smiling at me, not laughing or ridiculing, but simply smiling at me.

"'Hi Sunil!' Akash walked up to me and smiled.

"More than a little taken aback, I managed a "hi" and stood waiting for them to explain what they were doing at my house so early on a Sunday morning.

"Akash leaned in conspiratorially and whispered in my ears, 'Sunil, we are planning to go for a movie, would you like to join us?'

"Completely perplexed, I stared first at Akash and then at the others standing behind him to see if they were joking or trying to tease me, but they were all smiling and looking at me expectantly. 'I-I-I-I don't have money for the ticket,' I finally mumbled, not knowing what else to say, after all, in all the years that I had known these boys, they had never approached me for anything like this. All they had ever done was make fun of me and ridicule me.

"'Don't worry,' Akash said calmly. 'All of us will contribute towards buying you your ticket, okay? Just come. We'll leave in another half an hour, so meet us outside Karan's house.'

"I nodded my head and ran back inside the house, my mind still trying to understand exactly what had happened. I got ready in record time and ran out of the house some twenty minutes later, shouting out to my mother that I was going out with some of the *mohalla* boys and would be back later.

"I met the boys outside Karan's house, just as Akash had instructed, and together we all walked to the cinema hall near the main market. Akash bought seven balcony tickets from the money he had already collected. Since there was still some time left for the next show to start, we walked over to the small tea shop next to the hall and ordered a round of special tea.

"Over the next five minutes it became clear to me why I had been granted such special treatment by this gang of louts and bullies. Just as our tea was served on the table, Akash looked at me and, without beating around the bush, came directly to the point.

"'Who is the girl you were with last night, Sunil?'

"'Huh? Erm . . . Madhu,' I answered, wondering what this could possibly be leading up to.

"'How do you know her?' Akash shot another question.

"'She is my classmate,' I replied.

"'When there are so many other boys in your class, how does she know only you?' Akash persisted.

"It was then that I realised that there was something fishy going on. Akash was literally interrogating me!

"'Why are you asking me so many questions about Madhu?' I shot back.

"'We saw you both walking together last night, and it did not look like she is just a classmate,' Vikas offered, chuckling.

"Suddenly, Karan interrupted, 'She is not so easy to handle.'

"'What do you mean?' I asked.

"The boys had started sniggering and very punching Karan playfully. I was once again reminded of what I had seen when they had come back from the main market the day before. Akash silenced the boys and then, sipping his tea, he narrated the entire story.

"'We saw her in the market yesterday when we had gone to arrange food for you guys. When we crossed her, Karan here, passed a remark saying, 'Wow, *kya main din mein sapna dekh raha hoon*?' to which she immediately retaliated by saying, '*aur main din mein ullu dekh rahi hoon*!"

"All the boys burst out laughing now, Karan shifting around uncomfortably and looking very embarrassed, and I realised why he'd disappeared from his post at the temple gate the previous night when Madhu had appeared in the queue with her family.

"For the rest of the morning, even as we watched the film, I was constantly hounded by the boys with questions about Madhu. What was she like? What was her favourite colour? Her hobbies? Her likes? Dislikes? I was thoroughly fed up with their questioning. I hardly knew the girl, and what bond I was forming with her was also too new and too delicate to be picked apart like this. While I could understand that the boys were mostly curious, I could not help but hardly wait for the movie to get over. And the minute the words 'The End' flashed on the cinema screen, I was out of the hall like a shot. I didn't pay any heed to the boys calling out to me. I ran straight home and spent the rest of the day thinking about them, their questions, about Madhu, about our friendship, and what it meant when my heart raced every time she came near me.

"That night, long after dinner, long after everyone else in the house had gone off to sleep, I lay awake. Sleep eluded me. Every time I closed my eyes, Madhu's face came to my mind. Again and again and again. Was it just a crush, a teenage infatuation? Or was it love? I didn't know. I didn't have a single answer to any of the questions bouncing around in my head. Somewhere out in the distance, cutting through the pin-drop stillness of the night, came the sound of approaching thunder clouds. A dog barked somewhere, and I lay in bed, restless, waiting for the rain to fall, and for the questions in my heart to resolve themselves.

CHAPTER 6

"November crept up on me silently. Months had flown by, but I had not really noticed that because all my attention was focussed on Madhu. Our friendship had blossomed in the time that had gone by. From someone who had been appointed to help her out in catching up with studies, I had become her friend, someone who spent a lot of time with her, talked to her about everything, someone with whom she could share her thoughts and her feelings with. I had even taken to visiting her house in order to exchange notes and study together. Our parents too, were well aware of our friendship and approved of the good influence we had on each other for we were always studying and talking about sensible things. Madhu's mother, especially, was becoming quite fond of me.

"It was on the night of *Diwali* that things changed between me and Madhu.

"After completing the traditional Goddess Lakshmi *puja* first at our home and then at my father's shop in the main market, I walked over to Madhu's house to wish her and her family. *Diwali* meant gifts and new clothes for everyone, and like everyone else around, I was dressed in the new *kurta-pyjama* set my parents had gifted to me just that morning. When I reached Madhu's house, I found her father and her brother lighting up crackers and watching the fireworks.

"'Happy *Diwali*, Uncle. Happy *Diwali*, Ravi!'

"Both of them looked up at the sound of my voice and smiled on seeing me.

"'Happy *Diwali*, *beta*,' Uncle replied, beaming.

"'Happy *Diwali* Sunil *bhaiyya*!' Ravi exclaimed. 'Come light some crackers with me.'

"Nodding, I went and stood beside him, watching the *chakhri* run in dizzying circles in front of us and the *anaar* throw up a brilliant burst of sparks. After a couple of minutes, I turned to Uncle and asked him, 'Where are Aunty and Madhu?'

"'Inside, *beta*, they are busy lighting up *diyas* and finishing the *puja*. Why don't you go in and wish them as well? Your Aunty spent the entire morning making delicious food, am sure she will be more than happy to stuff you with *ladoos*.' Uncle patted my head and signalled to me to go right inside.

"I found Madhu's mother in the kitchen, busy putting the finishing touches on something she must have been cooking. 'Happy *Diwali*, Aunty!' I called out

"'Oh, Sunil!' she exclaimed when she turned around. 'Happy *Diwali* to you too, *beta*. May God bless you always.'

"'What are you cooking, Aunty? It's really smelling very good.'

"'Ah! I've been making special dishes all day for the *Diwali* dinner. It's almost ready. Why don't you also join us, Sunil?'

"'No, no Aunty. I just had an early dinner at home. My mother has also been cooking all day in order to make our favourite *Diwali* dinner. I am not hungry at all or you know I would never have refused your kind offer. I just came out to wish you all.'

"'Well then, go wish Madhu as well. She's in the backyard lighting candles.'

"Madhu was busy lighting up the candles that had been placed all along the backyard wall. Her back was towards me when I entered the backyard, and she did not see me standing near the door that opened to the backyard. For a full two minutes, I stood there, simply observing her quietly, the way she had left her hair open, the deep red of her *salwar kurta*, the tiny gold sequins on her *kurta* that sparkled and glittered and winked naughtily, the way the autumn breeze played with her *dupatta*, the way she flicked her hair back from her face while bending forward to light a candle. Very slowly and very quietly, I walked up to her and leaning forward, whispered in her ear, 'Happy *Diwali*, Madhu.'

"She recognised my voice which is why she didn't shriek or exclaim in response. She turned around slowly, and smiling beautifully, she wished me as well. 'Happy *Diwali*, Sunil. I didn't even hear you come in!'

"In the soft glow of the candles all around us and the *Diwali* lights that her father had strung up all over the house, Madhu looked exceptionally beautiful. Like an angel. She was standing so close to me that I could almost hear her heart beating. The sparkle in her eyes and the soft, warm flush on her cheeks were driving me crazy. The softness of her lips, like tender rosebuds, was making me lose control of my thoughts. And before I knew what was happening, my left hand was under her chin and I was pushing her face up towards mine, and then I was bending my head forward and bringing my lips close to hers and we were about to kiss under a starry sky with spectacular fireworks exploding all over behind us.

"But a fraction of a second before my lips touched hers, Madhu pushed me away and ran inside the house without so much as a word, leaving me alone to battle the deluge of questions and feelings and regret that attacked me a moment later.

Chapter 7

"Madhu had stopped talking to me after what had happened, rather, what had almost happened on *Diwali*. School had reopened after *Diwali* holidays and I tried, many many times, to talk to her in class, but she always managed to escape me. I was not sure how I was going to resolve this issue because Madhu was simply not giving me even a single opportunity to talk to her and try and explain things.

"Our school schedule had also changed a little bit. In order to give us ample time to prepare for our upcoming board exams, school timings for our class had been extended by two hours so that we could study more in the school premises itself. Our days became very tiring and hectic. All the studying and the preparation that was expected from us was strenuous, to say the least, but for me, it was doubly hard because I was worried about my friendship with Madhu.

"Then one fine day, we came to know that Yadav sir's father had passed away the night before which meant that he was on leave. Our Hindi period was therefore free. Though we were all sad to hear about Yadav sir's loss, the prospect of a free period also lifted the spirits of the class because it was the first time after two weeks of continuous back-breaking studying that we'd have some time to relax and do what we wanted. While almost the entire class decided to step out into the football field and enjoy the warm autumn sun, I was still wondering what to do when I saw Madhu pick up her books and head to the library to study.

"I had been on the lookout for yet another opportunity to talk to Madhu and I thought that perhaps cornering her in the library might give me the chance I needed to set things right. Then again, I had already tried so many times to talk to her and apologise and tell her about how I felt and what had happened to me that day, but she had rejected my efforts every single time. Beginning to feel a little hurt and angry, I thought to myself then that perhaps Madhu was being more than a little mean and unfair towards me. After all, did not our friendship mean anything to her? Did all the hours we had spent together and all the thoughts and feelings we had shared not mean that I deserved at least one chance to explain myself? She should not have ignored me like she had, I thought angrily. Why are girls always like this? I wondered, sad and upset. Why don't they think about the feelings of others? Angry, I decided not to follow Madhu into the library. If she wanted to talk to me, then she could come and talk to me. I would never ignore her and turn away from her, but I was not going to go chasing after her.

"With this thought in my head, I was about to storm out of the empty classroom and join my classmates on the football field when right at the door I bumped into Madhu, coming back from the library because she had forgotten something, her nose buried so deep in the book that she never saw me coming out of the classroom door. And I was so blind with anger that I didn't see her either.

"The pile of books in Madhu's hand fell and scattered at our feet when we collided.

"'Sorry! Sorry! I didn't see you coming!' I apologised, bending down to help her pick up her books.

"'Yeah, that's all right. I didn't see you too either . . .' she mumbled and quickly gathering her books, she started to hurry inside the classroom.

"Something about the way she avoided looking at me and hurried past, really hurt me and made me want to clear things out with her. I couldn't hold on to my anger. She was the best friend I had ever had and I couldn't let my anger come in between us.

"'Madhu, stop!' I said.

"'I am sorry,' I whispered when she turned around. 'I am sorry. I should have not done what I tried to do on *Diwali*. I am really sorry, Madhu, I do not know what came over me, but trust me, I regret it every single day. I don't want anything to spoil our friendship, Madhu . . .' I looked at her pleadingly, wishing she would say something, anything to put me out of my misery. If only she would forgive me, life would be all right once again!

"But Madhu didn't say anything for the longest time. Instead, she first fidgeted with her hands and then, walking up to her seat, she sat down quietly and stared at the pile of books in front of her. I stood where I was, by the classroom door, unsure whether to continue or not. One wrong move and I could very well lose Madhu forever.

"'It's all right,' she spoke up suddenly.

"I stared at her, startled, and then walking over to her seat, I sat down next to her. I could sense that she was a little uncomfortable talking to me about what had happened, but I also knew that we had to have this conversation if we were to protect our friendship. Very slowly, I then moved my hand and picked up her hand in mine. I expected her to snatch her hand back, to scold me, to shout at me, but she did not. Emboldened, I reached up to her face and lifted her chin up, forcing her to look at me. In the pin-drop silence of the empty classroom, I tried to look deep into her eyes and read her thoughts and assess her feelings, but I couldn't.

"'Madhu,' I mumbled, my voice shaking a little, 'I am not sure what you think about me now, but we were good friends before all of this happened and I want to continue being friends with you. Forever. We were good friends because we thought about each other, we cared for each other, and we are concerned about each other. When we have so many things in common, when we care so much, then how can our friendship be broken because of a single unwanted incident? How can we let our friendship just die like this?'

"Sensing no resistance from her I continued, 'Whenever I think about someone I would want in my life, someone I could fall in love with madly, I can only picture you, Madhu. You are always near me, even when we are not together. You are in my thoughts, my mind, and in my heart. Whenever I am happy, my heart tells me to celebrate the moment with you. When I am sad or distressed, I look for you because your presence gives me strength. That day, when I crossed my boundaries with you, I don't really know what happened and how it happened.

I only wanted to tell you how my heart races every time I see you, how you are all I can think about.'

I took a pause and continued.

'While you were out in the backyard, lighting all those candles, I was looking at you from the doorway and thinking just how beautiful and pure you are. And then, you turned towards me with your smile and I think the moment just became a little too overwhelming for me, and before I could think about what I was going to do, I ended up trying to put my love and my feelings into an act which somehow got misunderstood. Only after you ran and then stopped talking to me did I realise that I had acted rashly. I had not thought things through. Your silence forced me to snap out of my dreams. I have spent a lot of time thinking about everything and though I still don't know if this is what people call love, I know that I care very very deeply about you Madhu, and I will never do anything to hurt you. And if this is love indeed, then Madhu, I accept that I am in love with you. It is you, Madhu, who taught me to love . . .'

"I put my other hand on top of her hand and taking a deep breath, I said, 'Madhu, I love you. I love you from the bottom of my heart.'

"For a moment after the words were out in the open between the two of us, Madhu was still, absolutely still. Her eyes were closed and her breathing had quickened. I could hear the blood drumming in my ears. My heart was pounding so hard, it was almost painful. And though the chill of November meant that the weather was nice and pleasant, I was beginning to feel a little hot. Suddenly, Madhu stood up from her seat. I stood up instantly too, ready to stop her if she meant to leave without saying a word. She was looking very agitated and I saw that her eyes were a little moist. My words and my confession had clearly troubled her.

"'Madhu, you can't just leave me like this and walk away,' I said, knowing that unless I said something, she would just leave me and walk out of the classroom. 'You need to say something. Your silence is killing me, Madhu . . . I am unable to concentrate on anything else . . . I cannot go on like this, not knowing whether we are still friends, not knowing what you think, what you feel . . . please Madhu, say something!'

"Madhu looked up at me, the tears in her eyes glistening. 'Sunil,' she began after a heartbreakingly long moment, 'when I first came here and took admission in this school, in this section, I was not sure how the boys would react to a girl in their midst. I wondered whether I would make in friends in the class or not. I knew I would need help in catching up with everything that had already been taught. I was afraid of coming here, to a new place, and to a new school. But then, I found you. With you, I can discuss everything and anything, be it our studies, my feelings, my problems, my fears and my doubts, everything . . . some of the things I have shared with you are things I couldn't even bring myself to share with my mother! You are my best friend Sunil! Your presence makes me feel secure and comfortable. Not talking to you has been as difficult for me as it has been for you. I have become so used to sharing everything in my life with you that the past few days have been a painful experience for me as well. I don't know how and when all of this happened, how you have become so special for me, how you have come to mean so much in my life . . .' Madhu trailed off, shrugging her shoulders helplessly.

"'On that day,' she continued a moment later, 'it was not you, Sunil, who lost control, it was me. But I snapped out before things got too far. And I ran. I ran from you and I ran from that moment because I was afraid of myself, of what I was feeling. I couldn't trust my heart and I wanted to stop anything which could destroy our friendship from happening. I have spent a lot of time thinking about everything since then, Sunil, and I think it is too early for both of us to even consider something as big and as essential as love. This is too important a life decision for us to think about and make. We are young and immature right now. We need to study hard first and make our lives meaningful. Our parents have a lot of expectations from us. We need to fulfil them first. We owe our lives to them, Sunil. We must think about them and what they want from us and for us. If we let ourselves be swept away by all these feelings that are confusing us and occupying our thoughts, we will ruin our future. We cannot allow ourselves to be distracted by anything right now. We need to focus and concentrate on our studies so that we can do our best in the board exams and get excellent results. You need to support me and I need to support you as both of us prepare ourselves for the exams and for the future that lies ahead of us. We need to be each other's friends for now. Just that, Sunil. Do you love me? I know you do. And do I love you? You know I do. But are we feeling like this because of our age? That we do not know. Let's be more mature, more sure of ourselves and of our lives before saying anything further. Let time test our feelings for each other. Please Sunil, you have to understand me. I am so scared and I am feeling shakier than ever before. I have never been at such a loss before. I need your support and your help to figure things out. If you choose to part ways, I will understand, but I know I will not be able to recover myself from the loss of your friendship and your support . . . tell me Sunil, will you see us through this trying time or will you abandon me?'

"Time seemed to have stood still and all the small sounds drifting in from outside seemed to have grown louder. The birds chirping on the trees outside, the shrieks of the students playing on the field, a classroom door banging shut somewhere along the corridor . . . and the storm raging on inside my heart, I could hear everything with crystal clear clarity. Madhu stood in front of me, pleading silently with her eyes for me to understand her words and her thoughts. And I, I stood totally stunned. I had not a word I could give to her in comfort or in understanding. I had never thought of our relationship in as much depth and detail as she had. I was clueless about how I should react and what I could say, but I knew, even as my mind tried to understand everything that she had said, that she was right. Madhu was right about every single thing. I had not thought about the directions my immature desires were pulling me in. I had not thought of the consequences of my actions. I had not thought about my future, my career, about my actions and wants having an adverse impact on our lives and on the expectations of our parents. I had not thought about anything, and here I was, standing at a crossroad, getting tugged apart between my desires and what was clearly the right thing to do. I looked at Madhu, at that beautiful and intelligent girl in front of me, and the innocence on her face made me want to take her in my arms and kiss her. But I couldn't. Not after what she had said. Not after she had placed herself and her trust in my hands. I knew if I tried to kiss her then, in the middle of that empty classroom, she would not resist me. But I didn't.

"'I love you, Madhu,' I finally whispered, all my uncertainty and my love clear in my words. 'I want to hold you in my arms right now and kiss you, but I can't be so selfish that I wilfully disrespect your feelings. I need time to think about everything you just said, but I know you are right. I will always be your friend, Madhu, no matter what. We are best friends today and we shall be best friends tomorrow. But, Madhu, can I at least request you to think about us again after our exams are over? We do not have to rush into anything, but at least let us open up to the possibility of being more than best friends. It will also help us to know each other better and take a better thought-out decision later. But till then, I'll be your best friend . . . and Madhu, I am sorry about everything wrong that I have done till now.'

"'There is no sorry and thank you in friendship,' Madhu replied with a relieved smile.

"I smiled. She had just quoted the most famous line from the movie *Maine Pyar Kiya*. If there had been no movies then what would have happened to our lives? I wondered. Normally, its reel life that is believed to be driven by real life, but I always believed that it was vice-a-versa.

"'Come,' Madhu said, breaking my thoughts. 'Let's eat our tiffins before the recess is over. I am hungry. Aren't you?'

"I nodded happily, and we sat in that empty classroom, opening our tiffin boxes and sharing our lunches, talking about studies, cracking jokes, laughing, feeling better, happier. Like old times . . .

CHAPTER 8

"Life resumed its patterns over the next few months as both Madhu and I studied together for the upcoming board exams. The exams came and went in a flurry of hectic studying and revising. And when the results finally came out, Madhu was the school topper and I was second, my marks just a percentage less than hers. Both of us were happy with our results, though I knew that I owed my great result to Madhu and her wisdom which had stopped me from going astray.

"A couple of days after the result came out, once all the rejoicing at both our homes had calmed down a little, I told Madhu that we should reward ourselves for all the hard work we put in by going out and celebration. I asked her think of nice place we could go to, but for some reason, she did not look particularly interested in my idea. In fact, she looked quite distracted and unhappy about something. Dropping the idea of going out somewhere new and fancy, I told her that we could perhaps simply go and have tea at our school canteen.

She agreed readily and we walked over to the tiny canteen our school boasted of and ordered our canteen's special tea.

"'Madhu,' I turned to her, 'do you realise that this will be the last time we come here? This will be the last special *chai* we have in our school canteen! I didn't realise that until just this minute . . .' I trailed off, a little sad about leaving school.

"Madhu only nodded her head and walking to an empty table, she sat down. I paid for the teas at the counter and walked back with two steaming cups of special *masala chai* in my hands. 'Cheers for our success!' I said as I sat down and raised my cup to hers.

"Madhu only gave me a tight little smile and picking up her glass from where I had kept it on the table, she started sipping the steaming hot tea. This was strikingly odd because Madhu never drank hot tea. She would always let her tea grow tepid and only then would she drink, and that too in small slow sips.

"'What's the matter, Madhu? What happened?' I asked, unable to help myself from staring at her as she literally gulped down the tea.

"'Nothing . . .' she replied in between gulps.

"'Come on, Madhu. I know you well enough by now to know that there is something wrong. Look at the way you are finishing your tea! This is not the Madhu I know. You are not behaving like my Madhu.'

"'My father has been transferred to Mathura and we have to shift within the next two weeks,' she blurted out.

"'Whhhhat?' I almost shouted, standing up in shock, making my chair almost topple. Everyone in the canteen turned to look at me and realising that I could not possibly make a public scene and embarrass both myself and Madhu,

I waved my hand and said sorry before slowly sitting down again.

"'What are you saying, Madhu?' I asked her, my voice feeble.

"'You know,' Madhu began, avoiding looking at me, 'I always wanted to go to Banasthali for my graduation . . . now, with *Papa's* transfer it will be so much more convenient to attend Banasthali and also visit home without any problems.'

"'Madhu! What about me?'

"When she did not say anything, I banged my fist lightly on the table to catch her attention. 'Madhu! Answer me! What about me?!'

"A little startled by my vehemence, Madhu looked at me and said, her voice controlled, 'I think you need to look at your career and decide what you want to do from here on.'

"No, this could not be real. I shook my head, hoping the scene would change, that Madhu would go back to being the girl I loved, that she would be talking about us and our life ahead. But nothing changed and Madhu continued talking to me in her cold, controlled voice. 'Stop!' I interrupted her. 'Stop it, Madhu. You need to tell me where this leaves us. We need to talk about our relationship, Madhu. That is just as important as all these career things that you are talking about.'

"'I want to focus on my career right now, Sunil. This is the time to work hard and create a good life for ourselves. We need to focus on making our dreams come true.'

"'Madhu, I think you are taking our relationship very lightly. You are my future and I am yours and our relationship is what we should be focussing on. We spoke about all this only a few months back. Or have you forgotten that conversation, huh? You cannot just unilaterally decide something and leave me stranded like this in the middle of nowhere. You committed yourself to discussing our relationship and our future after our exams. That time is NOW!

"'In spite of our feelings for each other, we controlled our emotions and thoughts and focussed only on preparing for the exams. Our self control and our discipline have helped us in excelling in the exams. So, if we have done it in the past, we can do so again in the future. Why don't you understand Madhu that our relationship with each other is our strength? It will never ruin our future as long as we discuss our future together and make foolproof plans. We can achieve our dreams together. It is just a matter of aligning our dreams and committing ourselves to achieving them together.'

"'Sunil, you do not understand things. It is not so easy to just commit ourselves, not at this age. We need to concentrate on ourselves right now in order to fulfil our dreams and meet all our parents' expectations.'

"'We can do it, Madhu,' I persisted. 'I have full confidence in you and you have full confidence in me. We inspire each other to do better, don't we? Then what is there to stop us from achieving anything and everything together?'

"'No Sunil, you are blinded by your immature love. You are not thinking this through and you are definitely not being realistic.' Madhu got up and leaning forward, she said, 'Your responsibility right now is towards your parents. Fulfil the dreams of your family first, accomplish all that you can, and then, someday, I am sure, our paths will cross again and then, then we will talk about you and me and a life together . . . until then Sunil, pay your dues to your parents and to what is expected from you.'

"And with that, she left. I did not stop her even once. And she did not look back even once. My tea grew cold and I ordered another cup. And then that cup grew cold too. But I continued sitting there, lost in the pain and the confusion of knowing that my love had abandoned me to the twists and turns of life . . ."

Sunil stops speaking. The memory of that day in the school canteen has never stopped hurting him. But life has come a full circle for him. He has a loving wife and a beautiful daughter at home and all the love the world has to offers is his to enjoy. His memories of those days are still razor sharp and clear and sometimes he feels overwhelmed with all that he remembers. A little tired, Sunil looks down at his wristwatch and realises it's about to be twelve.

When Amit offers to make him a cup of coffee, Sunil nods his head and sinks back into his chair, using Amit's going inside to the kitchen as time to gather his strength and his memories in order to continue with his story.

Chapter 9

"Here's your coffee," Amit says, walking into the room.

"Thanks!" Sunil replies, taking the mug of coffee from Amit. He sniffs at the coffee appreciatively. "You know, I didn't realise that talking about myself would be tiring!" he quips.

"Haha!" Amit laughs, nodding his head. "Getting back to your story, Sunil," Amit looks at him sympathetically, "I can see that talking about all this still pains you a little, but your story has a spark. It has something which makes me want to know what happened next. Did you meet Madhu again? Or did she completely disappear from your life?"

"Ah!" Sunil grins. "If I tell you everything now, then what will happen to the rest of the story?"

"All right, all right!" Amit raises his hands in mock surrender. "Then why don't you just pick up the story from where you had left off?"

"Hmm . . . yes, of course," Sunil nods and settles himself comfortably, the cup of coffee balanced on his knee.

"After Madhu left, I made myself concentrate on thinking only about what I was going to do next. I was torn between joining an engineering college and learning the ropes of my father's business since I was the only son and it could be expected out of me to eventually take over the family business. Then, in last week of June, me and my entire family went to Lucknow to attend my cousin Anju's marriage. Anju is my *chacha's* daughter.

"I had always loved going to Lucknow. In fact, every year, we would make at least two-three visits to my *chacha's* house in Lucknow. The city always fascinated me. The sense of history and wonder that lurked at every corner of the city, especially the older parts, was extremely intriguing for a young boy from a small town. Being the political and cultural capital of Uttar Pradesh, Lucknow was always abuzz with activity and life, something or the other was always happening in Lucknow. However, in spite of being the nerve centre of Uttar Pradesh, Lucknow in fact entire Uttar Pradesh has always lagged a little behind in terms of development and progress. As a city it lacked the aggression which is so necessary to survive in this world . . . perhaps it was so because of the lingering traces of Awadhi history, for the city was steeped in Awadhi culture, be it the food or the mannerisms of the people, there was a grandeur and a slowness to things which can be fascinating at first, but which can also be a detriment for progress in the long run.

"Anyway, enough about Lucknow . . . when we reached *Chacha ji's* house—he lives in Rajajipuram which is a nice, well-planned colony in Lucknow— it was bustling with activity. With just two days left for the wedding, and with so many things still left to be done, everyone was all over the place. *Chacha ji* had gotten the entire front ground covered with a beautiful *shamiyana* and the tent house men were still fixing it up when we reached. After a lot of excited hugging and greeting at the gate, we were ushered inside where all the women of the family were busy fussing over Anju *didi*. The smell of a feast being prepared by the *halwai* in the backyard was all over the house.

"When everyone's attention shifted from the bride-to-be to me, I was congratulated by everyone and the elder members of the family gave their blessings and wished me success in life. *Chacha ji* slapped me on the back affectionately and asked, 'So Sunil, now that you got such an excellent result in your board exams, what do you want to do?'

"'I have not really been able to decide anything as of now, *Chacha ji*,' I replied honestly.

"'Hmm . . .' *Chacha ji* frowned a little, appearing a little unhappy with my indecisiveness. 'Tell me, Sunil, have you any specific aims in life?'

"'I-I-I want to be in business,' I replied a little hesitatingly.

"*Chacha ji* exchanged a look with my father. 'Sunil,' *Chacha ji* looked at me, 'I know, you want to get into business, but I think, and I am sure your father will agree with me, that you should first do some professional course and then you can decide whether you want a career in business or in whatever field it is that you do your graduation in. In fact, you can switch to a completely new field even after your graduation. You should keep all your options open, *beta*. I am not sure if you know this, but nowadays, computer professionals are very much in demand. My neighbour's son has recently gone to New York for a project. The IT industry is a goldmine of excellent opportunities. People get posted abroad for projects which means that you can travel the world. The pay is good and so is the work. In fact, Anju's would-be-husband, your *jija ji*, is also in the IT sector. He is working with Wipro and is posted in Bangalore. And only last week, he called me up to tell me that his company has asked him to go to Los Angeles for six months to complete a project there. He asked me to apply for Anju's passport! Why don't you consider the IT sector, Sunil? You already have an excellent science background. It should not be too difficult for you to handle it . . .'

"I looked across at my father and saw him nodding his head in agreement with *Chacha ji's* words. He then turned to me and urged me to consider his brother's advise. I looked around the room and everyone seemed to think that *Chacha ji* was right in asking me to consider IT as a career choice. No one seemed to remember that I had clearly stated that I wanted to get into business and eventually take over my father's business. But I trusted my parents and my elders and I knew they couldn't all be wrong. After all, they all only wanted the very best for me.

"'All right,' I said after a long moment of consideration that ended in giving in to my family's expectations. 'I will go for it. But,' I warned them, 'it is tough to get admission in an engineering college.'

"'Don't you worry about that,' *Chacha ji* assured me, looking relieved and happy. 'There are many good coaching centres in Lucknow and their results are also very encouraging. You can prepare yourself for the entrance exams and you can stay with us while you do the coaching. Only today morning, your *Chachi* was worrying about staying alone after Anju leaves for her in-law's house because I am on official tours at least once every month. She's always had Anju around to give her company. If you come and stay with us, it will keep her mind off things and I know she will be more than happy to take care of you.'

"*Chachi ji* nodded in my direction and smiled. '*Haan, beta*, your *Chacha* is right. You should come and stay with us,' she insisted. 'Lucknow has more opportunities for young people than Kalpi can offer. And a bright boy like you should be given all the chances possible to do well in life . . .'

"'It is decided then,' my father exclaimed happily, 'Sunil will come and stay here with you and do a year-long coaching and then sit for engineering entrance exams!'

"And thus was my fate sealed by my family and, like a free but helpless bird, I allowed myself to get trapped by their apparent happiness at having their expectations met.

CHAPTER 10

"About two weeks after Anju *didi's* wedding, I went back to Lucknow and started doing a basic round of research on the various coaching centres in the city. It was mind boggling to see how preparing for entrance examinations had become such a good business venture for some people. From early morning to late evening, batch after batch of eager students came rushing into the tiny, windowless classrooms these coaching centres provided and filled their copies and notebooks with furious scribbling, copying each word the teacher spoke. Every evening, *Chacha ji* and I would discuss what we had found out during the day, comparing coaching centres, matching one's advantage with the other, and finally, we settled on coaching classes taken by a Mr Manoj Kumar. He taught students in his house and not only did he come with strong recommendations from *Chacha ji's* friends, but the success rate of his students was also very good. Plus, his house was only two kilometres away from *Chacha ji's* house, so I'd save time and energy on travelling as well.

"Initially, I went walking, but within a few days, my uncle arranged an old bicycle for me and I also found out that one of the boys in the batch, Ajay, lived in the block next to *Chacha ji's* house. So both of us started cycling to the coaching class together. I settled into my new routine quite comfortably. Being at *Chacha ji's* house with *Chachi* taking such good care of me, I wasn't really missing my own home. Madhu's memories, however, did haunt me from time to time. For days I would go without thinking about her, and then suddenly, something small and ordinary would remind me about her and then I couldn't help but the feel the pain of the loss all over again. People say that it's not easy to forget one's first love, and it's true . . . letting go of Madhu and all her memories was no small task, but I knew that I had to focus on shaping my career.

"But Life has a mind of its own and with destiny as its partner in crime, it never shies away from playing tricks on us unsuspecting people.

"One day, about two-three months after my having shifted to Lucknow, *Chacha ji* went off on one of his official tours and it fell upon me to help *Chachi* around the house by doing all the chores that *Chacha ji* used to do.

"It was the first morning after my uncle's departure and *Chachi* had asked me to go and get fresh milk from a *doodhwala* who sat a few blocks away. 'Ajay's mother sends him there too, you can go with him, *beta*,' she had told me the evening before, and I had spoken to Ajay and told him to wait for me the next morning.

"'Welcome to fresh milk consumer union!' he chuckled when he saw me walking towards his house in the morning, an empty canister swinging from my hands.

"'Shut up!' I retorted.

"The place we were going to, the *doodhwala's* house, was in a small illegal colony of sorts which had sprung up along the sides of the chamfer that divided the two blocks of colony my *Chacha ji* lived in. Mornings saw a steady trickle of people making their way to this illegal colony of milkmen to collect fresh milk for the day's consumption.

"'There,' Ajay said, pointing to a small shack up ahead in the distance with a queue in front of it. 'That's where we are going.'

"I looked at the shack Ajay was pointing at and saw a girl come out with two canisters of milk, one in each hand. She was dressed in a pretty pink *salwar kameez* with a white *dupatta* draped loosely around her neck. She was slim and tall and even from a distance, I could sense a delicacy to her that was appealing. I craned my neck in order to see her face, but her hair, left loose, kept falling on her face and the early morning breeze was not helping her either, it kept whipping her hair around her face. Her head bent low, the girl walked slowly, as if trying to focus on the road in front of her while trying to see through the curtain of hair that shielded her face from my gaze.

"As we neared her, I slowed my steps, wanting to catch a glimpse of her face. When the girl was about three steps away from us, she stopped, kept the milk canisters down on the road, and with both her hands now free, she gathered her hair in a bunch and twisted it expertly into a bun at the back of her neck. Then, picking up the canisters, she crossed us and walked away.

"To say that she was beautiful to be an understatement. All this while, as she had taken care of her hair, I had stood with my mouth literally hanging open, as if it was a nymph, an angel descended from the heavens above who stood in front of me, an angel in her mortal, earthly avatar, loose strands of hair softly framing her beautiful face. My heart seemed to be pounding harder, faster, and blood thundered in my ears. I stood there frozen, wondering if she was for real, for how could anyone be so beautiful?

"Ajay had walked ahead without realising that I had stopped. When he turned around a second later, he found me not by his side, but a few steps behind, staring at the retreating back of the girl, my face bearing a rather stunned and stupefied expression. One look at me and Ajay understood the situation. He tried to pull me and make me walk towards the milk man's house, but I resisted, wordlessly staring at the girl, her delicate white *dupatta* fluttering in the wind behind her, until she turned a corner and disappeared from sight.

"'Come on, let's go now . . .' Ajay spoke up.

"When I turned to him he was smiling, but so enchanted was I with the vision of the girl that I didn't bother asking him why he was smiling. We reached the milk man's shack, got our canisters filled, walked back home, and the rest of the day went by in the same humdrum of daily life—food, studying, coaching, chores, tea, and food again. That night, however, after all the distractions of the day were gone, I found myself unable to study. All the symbols and the variable of the mathematical equation in front of me seemed to flow and disappear into the contours of the girl's face as I drew and redrew it from memory. I shook my head. I shut my eyes. I counted backwards from hundred to one, but nothing worked. My mind was determined to act like a wilful little boy. Exasperated with my own self, I shut my books and picked up a novel. Perhaps, I thought to myself, immersing myself in a fictional world would distract my mind from all thoughts of the girl. At any rate, there was no point in trying to work my way through Trigonometry when my mind clearly had its own agendas to fulfil. But even the novel failed to work. As did my attempt to sleep a little later. And I tossed and turned for what turned out to be the possibly longest night of my life, falling asleep only at around four in the morning.

"Needless to say, when I woke up the next morning at around half past seven—a little later than my usual time—my eyes were red and burning and crying out for a few more hours of sleep and I had an unbearable headache that made me want to claw out my hair. I felt cranky and irritated, not to add that I looked like someone who had been put through a washing machine dryer.

"When I walked into the kitchen, my aunt took one look at my face, and hurried over, feeling my forehead with her hands to check if I was running a temperature. I hastened to reassure her that I was all right, and that it was just a headache and the lack of sleep which were making me look so exhausted.

"'Sit sit,' Chachi nodded towards the single chair next to a small table kept in the kitchen. 'I will give you some *garam chai*. That should help your headache. And *beta*, take it a little easy today. Too much of studying is also not good. You need to give yourself small breaks from time to time, okay?'

"I nodded and sat down, and for the next quarter of an hour, I gave myself up to the easy bantering of my aunt as she went from one domestic topic to another, telling me family stories and bringing me up to date with family news. The homeliness of the scene reminded me of my mother and I found much comfort in the warmth of the kitchen.

"At around 9:30 a.m., Ajay rang the doorbell to the house to go for the coaching class. I had been contemplating about not going and resting for one day, but since Ajay was already there at the door, I decided to quickly get ready and go anyway.

"'So, did you get a good night's sleep?' Ajay asked after we had left the house and were cycling towards our class.

"Surprised by his question, I turned and looked at him. He was grinning, and it appeared as if he knew something, but wasn't telling me. When I didn't answer his question and continued paddling my cycle, Ajay repeated the question again. This time, I gave him a seriously furious look and without a word, cycled faster and put some distance between the two of us. Ajay did not attempt to catch up with me and when eventually he took his seat next to me in the classroom, I refused to either look at him or speak to him. Once done with the class, I got up hurriedly and was about to walk away when Ajay stopped me and asked me to accompany him to his house. 'There's something important that I need to discuss with you,' he said. The seriousness on his face somehow convinced me to agree to his request and we cycled over to his house. On the way, he told me that his family had gone to Aminabad for the day to do some *Diwali* shopping and that they would only come back much later in the evening so he is alone for whole day.

"'Would you like to have a cup of tea?' Ajay asked when we had reached his house and he had ushered me in to the well-kept drawing room.

"'Why not,' I said, plonking down on a sofa and keeping my bag next to me.

"Ajay nodded and disappeared into the kitchen inside. I followed him a minute later and stood by the kitchen door, watching him put the water on boil in a stainless steel saucepan. Stirring in some sugar and milk into the sauce pan, Ajay started talking to me while he waited for the water to boil. 'Sunil, I am registering myself to DOEACC 'O' level.'

"'What? Why?' I asked, surprised. In our numerous discussions about studies and future plans, the possibility of doing DOEACC had never once come up. Therefore, I was quite surprised with Ajay's decision.

"'You know just how tough the competition for engineering seats in our state is, and every year, the huge gap between the number of seats available and the number of students competing for these seats only widens. There is a good possibility that we might not get a seat this year. Or the next year either. It's not negative thinking, but it's just a question of supply and demand. We cannot keep taking coaching classes every year either. I spoke to my cousin and he suggested that I do this. It will not only avoid another year's loss, but it will also help me fulfil my career aspirations.'

"'Hmm . . .' I pondered over what Ajay had just said. 'Good thinking, for sure . . .' I said.

"'Do you also want to register?' Ajay asked suddenly. 'It will give us the opportunity to study together . . . it's a tough course after all. We'll need a lot of disciplined self study,'

"'I haven't thought about all this . . . so I don't know to be honest. Also, I can't decide things so fast like you. Give me some time, I'll think it over and also discuss it with *Chacha ji* and then tell you,' I replied, smiling.

"'All right. I will give you the brochure so that you can get a better idea of things before you take a decision.'

"I nodded and we stood silently in the kitchen, watching the tea come to a boil as bubbles erupted near the surface and burst open before bubbling up again. Ajay was pouring out the tea into two cups when the telephone rang in the drawing room. Since he was busy, he asked me to go pick it up. Since I knew almost everyone in his family and relatives, I was also not hesitant to pick it up.

"'Hello?' I spoke into the receiver half a minute later.

"'Hello, may I talk to Aunt?' a girl's voice spoke softly from other end.

"'She isn't here actually. May I know who this is?' I inquired.

"'Umm . . .' the girl hesitated. 'Is this Ajay *bhaiyya*?' she asked.

"'No, no, I am Sunil, Ajay's friend.'

"'Oh, okay . . . I am Sonali . . .'

"'Okay. Should I call Ajay?'

"'Yes, please.'

"'All right then, just give me a minute.'

"'Thanks Sunil!'

"I hurried back to the kitchen after putting receiver down. 'It's some Sonali asking for your mother,' I told Ajay. 'I told her she isn't here. Now she wants to talk to you.'

"Ajay nodded and quickly left the kitchen with a rather mysterious smile on his face. I put the two cups of tea on a tray and looked around for some biscuits and *namkeen* to munch on with the tea. When I finally entered the drawing room a little while later with the tray in my hand, Ajay had just finished the call and was putting the receiver down. I kept the tray on the centre table in the drawing room and sat down on a chair in front of Ajay. I gestured to Ajay to pick up his cup of tea, and picking up one myself I sat back and sipped on the tea, thinking about what Ajay had told me about DOEACC. After a while I got the feeling that Ajay was staring at me and when I looked up I found that indeed he was staring at me with that same mysterious, mischievous smile on his face which I had spotted earlier.

"'What happened?' I asked, slightly irritated.

"'Nothing.' Ajay replied, shrugging his shoulders and continuing to sip his tea.

"'What happened to you yesterday?' he asked a little later.

"'Huh? Yesterday? Nothing happened to me yesterday.' I replied, slightly confused by his question.

"'Come on . . . did you sleep at all last night? Or did the morning's experience leave you feeling strange?' he persisted.

"'Morning's experience? It was okay . . . not something I would like to do every day though" I replied cautiously, indicating that I thought he was asking about the milkman.

"Ajay continued sipping his tea and did not pursue his line of questioning any further. I stayed silent as well, not willing to talk about my experience at all.

"'Sunil,' Ajay broke the silence, 'remember you once asked me if there was some way you could earn some extra pocket money? Well, I have a proposal for you. Can you give tuitions to a Class 8 student?'

"'Hmm . . .' I thought about the idea for a minute. 'I can, but not right now. *Diwali* is coming up and I will be going home for at least a week and no one would want to pay a tutor for such a long holiday and that too so soon after starting.'

"'True, but think again. You may not get such a good opportunity again. I know the family personally and they are very good and generous people. You'll be suitably compensated for your efforts,' Ajay said.

"'Tuitions are easy to come by, Ajay. I do not think that we should really worry about my missing this particular one. I like your idea of taking tuitions, but perhaps I can start it after I come back from Kalpi? After all, every parent wants good marks for their kids, and because no one really has the time to take care of their children's studies, tuition teachers are always in demand,' I replied.

"'Hmmm,' Ajay thought over my words. 'I have an idea, something which will work out both ways. Let me take this particular tuition up for a month and once you are back from home, you can take it over. This will help you not to miss this chance and it will also keep the parents of this child satisfied that their child is getting the necessary guidance,' Ajay suggested.

"'That's a great idea!' I nodded my head in agreement and after that we spoke of various other things before I finished my time and left for home.

"I left for Kalpi about two weeks after that. As the hustle-bustle of Lucknow gave way to the quieter ways of a small town, I found myself glad to be back in the town where I had grown up. Nothing had changed in my absence for I had hardly been gone a couple of months, but I looked at everything with great fondness, as if I were memorising details lest I forget them. My mother's cooking tasted better than ever before, my sister's naughtiness sweeter, and my father's seriousness more endearing. Even Diwali seemed prettier. Everything came with the pinch of knowing that I would leave it all within a few days and go back to the noise and pollution of Lucknow.

Chapter 11

"It was a couple of days after my return from Kalpi that Ajay took me to the house where I was supposed to take tuitions. It was quite near my *Chacha's* house and when I saw it, I realised that I had crossed it many times on my way to Ajay's house and I had often seen a thirteen-fourteen-year-old boy playing football in the garden outside all by himself. It was probably that same boy to whom I was expected to give tuitions to.

"There was no one outside when we entered the compound through the main gate. Crossing the garden, we walked up to the main door and Ajay knocked on it while I stood beside him, slightly nervous.

"A couple of minutes later, we heard the sound of someone running to the door and then drawing back latch. When the door opened, I saw that it was the same boy who I usually spotted playing outside. He greeted Ajay with familiarity and ushering us in, he went inside to call his mother.

"I looked around the drawing room while we waited for the boy to return with his mother. A very nicely done up room, it gave me a good idea about the family's good taste and prosperity. Everything was simple but beautifully kept and maintained. I was just about to ask Ajay how he knew the family when a woman dressed in a pale yellow *chikankari* suit entered the room. And walking behind her was the same girl I had seen that distant morning when I had been going to fetch milk for my aunt. Dumbfounded, I stared at her for a full minute before I told myself that it was rude and I better mind my manners.

"'*Namaste* Aunty,' Ajay was saying as he stood up and greeted the woman.

Following his lead, I stood up too and greeted the woman respectfully, being careful to keep my eyes averted from the girl.

"'*Namaste beta*,' the woman responded with a smile and gesturing us to resume our seats, she and the girl came and sat down in front of us. After that, what followed was an exchange of basic information, where the woman first asked me questions about myself—where was I from? What subjects had I studies? What was I doing now? etc. etc.,—and I answered the best I could, distracted as I was with the girl's presence, before she went on and told me about herself and her family.

"'My husband, Mr S. K. Sharma,' she said, 'is a civil contractor. He works mostly with the Irrigation department and picks up contracts for the laying of water pipelines, and digging tube wells and open channels. I am a home-maker and an active member of the local ladies club. We have two children. Sonali, here, is studying in the twelfth standard and is a commerce student, and Sanket, your student, is in eighth standard. Both of them are studying in the City Montessori School . . .' she paused for a moment and smiling, continued, 'so that's all you need to know about us. Ajay has told me already that you are a good, hard working student and I am happy, *beta*, that you are going to help Sanket out. I'll expect you to start from tomorrow itself, all right?'

"We left soon after that. Things had started clicking and falling together in my mind—the first time I saw Sonali; her telephone call when I had been at Ajay's house; Ajay's mischievous smile; his persistently asking me about the day I had first seen Sonali; his insistence on me taking up Sanket's tuition. Ajay knew about my crush on Sonali and he did not want me to miss an opportunity to be around her and get to know her better! That's the reason he had worked out this foolproof plan to not only help me get extra pocket money, but also perhaps actually connect with someone who had literally stolen my peace and left me sleepless!

"'So, are you happy now, Sunil?' Ajay asked the minute we were out of the gate.

"'Ya,' I mumbled, not willing to admit to my happiness at this unexpected gift.

"'I deserve a party, you know,' he said, chuckling.

"I looked at him and shrugged before looking away.

"'Not right now,' he continued, 'but when you get your first payment, then.'

"'Cool,' I replied calmly, still not willing to let him know that I was mentally thanking God for giving me this chance. I did not know what life held in store for me, but this opportunity to try and get to know someone was a blessing. While I knew I would never be able to completely forget Madhu, I was ready to make a fresh start and risk my heart again.

* * *

"It was Sonali who opened the door and led me in to Sanket's study room the next day when I rang the doorbell dot on time. I had spent most of the day checking my watch again and again to keep track of time so that I won't be late. I hadn't spoken a word to her the previous day, and apart from smiling politely at her as she left me in Sanket's study room, I did not try to interact with her immediately.

"The study room, I saw, had actually been a small veranda that had now been covered and converted into a small room nicely fitted with a study table, two comfortable chairs, a book shelf, and a table lamp. Sanket came in a minute later and because it was my first day, I asked him to show me the topics that had already been covered by Ajay earlier. I also tried to gauge an understanding of his interest levels in the various subjects I was expected to teach him so that I could work out a schedule and prioritise lessons accordingly. Sanket was a bright boy and I realised that he could do very well with the slightest bit of guidance from me, but, like other boys his age, he had a very low concentration level and I found him eager to get out and play. Half an hour into the class, Sanket's mother walked in with a cup of tea and a plate of biscuits on a tray, and though I politely said no when she kept the tray in front of me, she insisted on me eating something at least, saying that young boys needed to eat in order to grow. I picked up the cup of tea and a single biscuit and thanking her politely, I told her that she should not do this daily. Smiling, she dismissed my formality and left us to our books.

"An hour later, done for the day, I was crossing the drawing room on my way out when I found Sanket's mother sitting there, having a cup of tea with a man who looked quite like Sanket and talking quietly. Must be Sanket's father, I thought to myself. When he saw me, Sanket's father beckoned me to come and sit down with them. I greeted him politely and quietly sat down on one of the sofas.

"'So, Sunil, how is your coaching going on?' he asked.

"'Fine, Uncle,' I replied.

"'And are you comfortable dividing your time between your coaching, your self-study, and this one and a half hour tuition? I hope this will not disturb your own studies.'

"'Not, at all. I am confident of being able to manage things properly. Normally, I keep this time of the evening free, so I don't think there will be any issues as far as time management is concerned,' I assured him.

"'I like your confidence,' he said, and turning to his wife, he smiled and said, 'I don't think we need to worry about Sanket's studies anymore.'

"'Yes, I know.' Sanket's mother nodded her head in agreement and smiled at me. 'I spoke to Sunil yesterday and found him confident and capable of handling Sanket, otherwise I would have asked Ajay to continue with the tuition.'

"I smiled on hearing such good words being spoken about me, and taking their leave, I left the house feeling good about myself. Almost a week passed before I thought it appropriate to ask Sanket about Sonali. In all the days that I had been coming to take the class in the evening, never once had I seen Sonali except for the very first day when she had opened the door for me.

"'Where is your *didi*, Sanket?' I asked him.

"'Must be in her room,' he mumbled. 'She stays there only all the time, studying and doing homework. I always get scolded because of her being such a bookworm,' he complained.

"'Hmm . . . you should also study hard like your *didi*. No one is stopping you from playing, but you should fix a time for playing and studying. You cannot only stand outside and play football all the time, Sanket,' I advised him. For the rest of the class, I did not mention Sonali again, thinking it better to not sound too eager to talk about her.

"A week later, I found an entire bunch of women in Sanket's house when I got there for the tuition class. Turned out that it was Sanket's mother's turn to host the monthly kitty party. It was difficult for me to keep Sanket engaged in the lesson that day as he was naturally distracted with all the noise and the laughter that was coming in from the drawing room where the women were talking. It was only towards the end of the class when the noise level began to go down a little until finally, there was pin drop silence. But the day had been more or less wasted. A little disappointed, I wrapped up the lesson and was just about to leave when Sonali walked into the study room and told me to wait in the drawing room for a moment before leaving. Her sudden entrance into the study room and her peculiar request had thrown me a little off balance and I had been unable to either say anything or ask her why she wanted me to wait in the drawing room. I had simply nodded my head as she turned around and left the room.

"When I made my way to the drawing room a minute later, Sonali was nowhere to be seen. The drawing room itself was a mess, with used plates and glasses kept on the centre table, the cushions all awry, and a couple of extra chairs added here and there. I sat on one of the sofas as I waited for Sonali, slightly fidgety, trying to leaf through a magazine to distract myself. We hadn't exchanged a word all this while, so what did she suddenly want from me? Why had she asked me to wait? Sanket had left to play football the minute I had finished the lesson. My preaching has not at all made any change in him. Were Sonali and I alone in the house? A hundred questions were attacking my head while I waited for her.

"Finally, after what seemed like hours, Sonali entered the drawing room with a tray laden with food in her hands.

"'My Mom told me to make sure you eat whatever was prepared for the party today before you left,' she said as she kept the tray down on the table in front of me, thus explaining why she had asked me to wait.

"'Oh! That's really nice of her,' I mumbled, feeling a little shy. Unsure of what to say next, I looked at all the food in front of me. There was *idli*, *dhokla*, *chhole kulcha*, *gulab jamun*, *namkeen*, and a cup of tea. Clearly, Sonali's mother had gone all out for her party.

"'Your mother must have been cooking all day to prepare such a feast,' I remarked after a moment. Smiling, Sonali just nodded her head. 'Where is she? I can't see her anywhere,' I continued, encouraged by her smile.

"'She has gone to the market with Ajay *bhaiyya's* mother,' Sonali replied.

"'Hmm . . .' I nodded my head, wondering what to say next. I wanted to keep talking to Sonali, but I didn't know what to say. 'And, ahem, how is your study going on?' I asked finally as an uncomfortable silence threatened to break out between us.

"'It's going quite well, sir,' I cringed when I heard her address me as 'sir'. Even Sanket didn't call me sir!

"'Please do not call me sir,' I told her immediately.

"'What should I call you then?'

"'Sunil. You can call me by my name.'

"She nodded her head and smiled and gestured to me to pick up a plate and eat something. So I picked a plate took a helping of the *chhole, kulcha* and the *idli* before looking at her questioningly. 'Won't you eat something?' I asked.

"'No,' she shook her head. 'I've already had enough earlier.'

"I nodded and began picking at the food, eating as slowly as possible as I wanted to prolong the moment.

"'The food is very very tasty,' I said after having taken a few bites.

"'My mother is a great cook,' Sonali replied in a matter of fact manner.

"I smiled. 'So, what is your favourite dish?'

"'Ah!' Sonali smiled happily. 'I love everything that Mummy makes! My favourite is South Indian food and trust me, she makes excellent *dosas*!'

"'I am sure she does. I will have to try and make her treat me to her *dosa* some day!' I joked. Sonali was clearly becoming more comfortable in talking to me and that gave me courage to continue the conversation further. Over the next couple of minutes I asked her about her hobbies, her likes, dislikes, her favourite subjects, etc. and found myself wanting to know more and more about this beautiful girl sitting in front of me. The bright yellow of the top she was wearing added a sparkle to her eyes that I found unable to look away from and her voice was so sweet and so melodic that I wished it would never stop. I was almost done eating when her mother walked in and seeing her, I snapped back to attention.

"'Aunty,' I stood up, smiling, 'Sonali told me that you asked her to make sure I ate some of this tasty food before I left, thank you so much! Everything is awesome, so delicious that I think I overate. I won't need dinner tonight I think.'

"'Thank you, *beta*,' she replied.

"We chitchatted for a couple of minutes and then I left, bidding both Sonali and her mother a polite good bye.

"And that night, once again, Sonali's face captured my mind and sleep was lost to me.

Chapter 12

"I met Sonali multiple times over the next few months, but our encounters were brief and our conversations were limited to a 'Hi! How are you? How are your studies going on?' Given that I was Sanket's tuition teacher, this was but natural, but the very limited nature of my interactions with Sonali had begun to frustrate me. I wanted to know her better, and for her to know me better, but there was simply no opportunity for either of us to sit down and talk. Life, however, has strange tricks up its sleeve and all this changed when one day, right out of the blue, Sonali's mother asked me to pick up Sonali from the centre for her last exam as it was in Alambagh, which was quite far from the house, and as her husband was also not there to pick up Sonali himself, he had left town on some urgent business work. The exam was going to start at three in the afternoon and would end by six in the evening, and she did not want Sonali to travel alone all the way from Alambagh. Needless to say, I was delighted to accept her request, and on the day of the exam, I was there at the gate of the exam centre dot at six in the evening.

"When the students started walking out a couple of minutes later, I noticed that almost all of them looked happy. No wonder, I thought to myself, its their last exam after all. Many were cheering and high-fiving each other. Looking at them, I could remember how I used to feel relieved and happy after my last exam. When Sonali came out eventually, she too looked very relaxed and happy. When she saw me, she smiled and walked over to where I was waiting.

"'Hi Sunil!' she greeted me. 'Thank you so much for picking me up.'

"'No problem at all, Sonali,' I smiled and reassured her.

"'I am very thirsty, Sunil,' she said. 'Do you think we have time to grab a quick glass of juice at the juice stall across the road?'

"'Sure thing,' I nodded enthusiastically, 'but call your mother first and take her permission as we may get delayed by half an hour at least.'

"'Hmm . . .'

"We looked for a PCO nearby and when we finally found one, Sonali called her mother and took her permission to stay out until a little later than usual since her exams were all over. Permission granted, we walked over to the juice stall and ordered two glasses of mixed fruit juice before settling down at one of the empty tables outside the stall. It was a small roadside place, bustling with customers and activity. Apart from the noise of the traffic, the sound of the juicer continuously grinding away fruit pulp to make juice meant that unless one sat very close to one's companion, conversation would almost be impossible. It was not an ideal place to meet someone you had a crush on, but things are not always to one's liking. Sonali and I sat silently for the next five minutes, both of us staring at the constant flow of traffic on the road in front of us. A small boy came and served us our two glasses of juice and left and still we said nothing.

"'How was your exam?' I finally broke the silence after taking a sip of the juice.

"'It was great actually, much better than I had expected . . .' she replied.

"'That's good,' I smiled. The ice was breaking between us and I could see Sonali beginning to be a little more comfortable. 'So what is your plan now?' I asked.

"'Hmm . . . I want to go for a BBA first and then do MBA,' she replied confidently.

"I was impressed with her clear thought and determination. 'Any specific reason why you want to study business administration? Why not CA?' I asked.

"'Umm . . . I am not very good with numbers, and in CA, one has to deal with too many numbers, that's why no CA. But as for why I want to do BBA, I guess it's because business has always interested me.'

"'Hmmm . . .'

"'And you, what about you? Why engineering?' she asked me now.

"'I think, I am good at it, it appears to be absolutely fitted for me!' I chuckled.

"She stared at me for a quick second before smiling and picking up her glass.

"'So,' I asked a moment later, 'what are your plans for the summer vacations? You are free now until the admission forms for colleges start coming out, isn't it?'

"'Yes, I am free . . . perhaps I'll join a music class somewhere. I am not sure yet, haven't had the time to really think about this since I was busy studying for the exams until now.'

"'Music class, huh? That's a great idea.'

"'How is your coaching going on? Ajay *bhaiyya's* mother had come over a few days back. I overheard her telling Mummy that the work load has increased now.'

"'That's true,' I nodded my head. 'The entrance exams are almost round the corner now, and I am trying very hard to pick up the momentum as it is very important for me to get through an engineering college this year itself. I cannot afford to lose another year preparing for the entrance exams. I have to crack it this year.'

"'I am sure, you will manage it.'

"'Hmmm . . . but how can you say that with such confidence?'

"'Well, I always believe in hard work and giving whatever we do our best, and I have seen you putting your best effort in teaching Sanket. Also, Ajay *bhaiyya* has often spoken about your diligence and your dedication. That's why I think you will accomplish your dream, Sunil.'

"'Thanks for the compliments, Sonali . . . but, honestly, I think that sometimes you need to be lucky as well. It's not easy to get through an engineering college in our state. There are way too many students appearing for the entrance exams and there are way too less seats for them. With everyone taking coaching and working just as hard, if not more, to pass these exams, it's not only hard work that I need but a bit of luck also to pass these exams.'

"'Sunil, don't be pessimistic. If you believe in hard work, you can change your destiny even if it is not in your favour. You alone have the power to change things and turn them around to your favour. That's what I believe.'

"I stared at Sonali with surprise. Her confidence was not only amazing, but it was motivating as well. She was almost a year younger to me, but it was clear to me that she had a much better outlook on life than I did. 'Sonali, I must say that I am really impressed with your confidence. You have really motivated me to have a little more faith in my own self. I know that my preparation has been up to the mark till now, but your words have inspired me to put in yet more effort!'

"'Hmm . . . but you know Sunil, it is easy to preach and difficult to practice. Here I am, telling you to have a little more confidence in your ward work, but I myself feel scared and unsure about my future every time I think about the MBA I want to go for. Getting through the CAT exams is so very difficult. Whenever I think about it, my heart sinks.'

"'But Sonali, every time I have seen you at your house, I have always found you studying something or the other. I am sure your preparation is excellent, and with what you just told me about hard work, I am pretty sure that you yourself will definitely get what you have aimed for.' I could see that Sonali was beginning to get a little tense. Clearly, even the mention of her CAT exams was enough to make her nervous and scared. I didn't want to upset her, instead, I wanted to help her gain confidence and do well in her career. Suddenly, an idea hit me. 'Sonali,' I said excitedly, 'I have a brilliant idea for both of us.'

"'What idea?'

"'Well, like you just said, it's easier to preach than to practise, so we are better at inspiring someone else with confidence than inspiring our own selves and having more confidence in our work. So, why don't we become preacher for each other? You preach to me, and I preach to you! This way both of us will be motivated and this will help us to concentrate better on preparing for our exams.'

"'That's an excellent idea, Sunil!' Sonali exclaimed with delight.

"And that was how I laid the foundation of my friendship with Sonali. I was not sure whether what I had just proposed would last or not, but I was willing to give it my best shot for I wanted to use every opportunity I had to get to know her better, to increase the depth of my fledgling relationship with her. We sat at the juice stall for a little while longer. Sonali spoke about a lot of things and as she talked, I sat next to her, dreaming about a life together, about her and me, about our futures. As I stitched together the images of a life with her, I knew some of my dreams and expectations were both unrealistic and impractical, but I did not want to stop. I did not want to tell my heart to put a break on its imagination. We finished our fruit juice, I paid the shopkeeper, we found an auto to take us home, we sat through a traffic jam, I dropped her home, wished good night to her and her mother, I walked back home, had dinner, and retired for the day, and all the while, my heart soared with hope and love.

Chapter 13

"Soon after what I came to consider my first unofficial date with Sonali, I devoted myself entirely to the last phase of my studies for the entrance exams. I had already finished Sanket's syllabus and I now stopped going for the tuition classes and confined myself to coaching classes in the morning and self-study at home. With the entrance exams just round the corner, I could not afford to waste my time doing anything else. My encounters with Sonali also lessened as a result of the change in my daily routine. The only time I now saw her was when she came to the ground next to my *Chacha's* house to practise driving the new Kinetic scooter her father had purchased for her. Father and daughter would arrive at the ground in the evening time, their driving sessions coinciding with the time I had allotted myself for a tea break which I almost always took sitting in the lawn outside *Chacha's* house. She would go round and round the ground, her father sitting behind her, guiding her and telling her what to do. She would smile when she saw me and her father would nod at me and I would smile and nod back. That was the extent of our interaction. I was happy just to be able to see her. And it was entertaining too, to see her learn how to drive. Within two weeks, Sonali had become more confident of her driving. Her father stopped accompanying her and she would drive around the ground on her own.

"Only once did I talk to her in this period. It was when she drove over to our house with a packet of sweets. Sanket, she told me, had passed his exams with flying colours, scoring a ninety-five percent in all. Her mother had asked her to deliver the sweets and thank me on her behalf for guiding Sanket and teaching him. She stayed back for a quick cup of tea and left soon after as my exams were less than a week away and I was too occupied with studying to do anything else.

"I had been banking on doing the last phase of preparation with Ajay, but his sister-in-law was expecting and hence he had gone to Muzaffarnagar with his entire family. In fact, he had chosen Muzaffarnagar as his exam centre. Left all to myself, I found myself getting overwhelmed sometimes by all that was at stake, but, keeping Sonali's words in mind, I would shrug my doubts off and go back to studying and preparing for the upcoming exams.

"Just two days before my exam, a heavy rain storm hit Lucknow in the night. I was studying in my room, literally burning the midnight oil as they say, when the storm began. The wind howled outside my window, making the tree right outside lash against the glass window like a whip. When the rain started, I could hear the drop falls on the tin roof of the garage shed outside. The clap of thunder that came a little later was a shock to me, making me almost jump right out of my chair. The electricity went off a little later. I groped around the table for the emergency candle in the drawer. I found it buried under some of my sample test papers. I studied in the candlelight for the next two-three hours as the storm continued raging with a mad fury outside. The electricity eventually came back around half past two in the night I think. When I finally went to sleep at around four-thirty in the morning, it was still raining and it was pitch dark outside. I got up at around ten in the morning and found that though the rain had stopped, everything outside wet and muddy. The window in my room overlooked the garden and I could see that the storm had wreaked havoc with my *Chachi's* carefully and lovingly maintained garden. When I walked out of my room, I found my uncle at home and both he and *Chachi* appeared ready to go somewhere.

"'How come you are at home, *Chacha ji*? Are you going somewhere?'

"'Yes, yes,' he replied, looking a little upset, 'one of my friends was hospitalised last night so we are going there to visit him.'

"'Oh all right, I hope it's nothing serious. When will you be back? Evening?'

"'Not sure, Sunil. Depends on the situation there. We might come back very late in the night or we might not come back until tomorrow.'

"'Oh!' I was more than a little surprised by *Chacha ji's* response. Most of the good hospitals in Lucknow were not far from his house which meant that there was no real need for him not come back at all. He could always come back to home and then go to the hospital again if the need arose.

"'Sunil, your breakfast is kept in the kitchen. Please make yourself a cup of tea and have it along with the breakfast. I have asked Sonali's mother to take care of your lunch and dinner because I don't want you to waste your time cooking or going out,' *Chachi* told me.

"They left after that and locking the door behind them, I hurried through my morning rituals and sat down to have breakfast. *Chachi* had made my favourite stuffed *parathas* and I sat in the veranda next to the dining room, looking out at the rain-washed greenery outside and enjoyed my breakfast. I was just thinking of making a cup of *adarak chai* for myself when the door bell rang. When I opened the door, it was Sonali. She had parked her kinetic right outside the gate and was standing at the door, dressed in a lovely white top and a pair of blue jeans, with a beautiful smile on her face. I gawked at her for a full moment before I remembered to smile back and usher her in. She was carrying a bag in her hand and when I offered to carry it in for her, she shook her head and walked in before me, heading straight to the kitchen. A little perplexed, I shut the door and was about to walk in into the kitchen when she came out carrying a flask and two empty cups.

"'*Chai*!' she said, gesturing towards the flask with a smile.

"I smiled back. So her mother must have sent her here with the food, I thought to myself. 'I was just having my breakfast in the veranda,' I said. 'Lovely weather . . . why don't we sit outside and enjoy our cups of tea?' I asked.

"'Sure, why not!' she nodded her head in agreement.

"I led her to the veranda and once she was seated, I sat down next to her. Up close, I could see that her hair was still slightly wet. She must have just showered and come over. She smelt of roses and spring and I couldn't help but draw in a deep breath, filling myself up with her presence.

"'How is your preparation going on?' Sonali asked, breaking my thoughts.

"'I think it's going on well, but only the final result will decide just how well it actually was,' I replied.

"She handed me a cup of tea and smiled.

"We finished our tea in companionable silence and Sonali left after that. I went back to room to resume my studying and worked my way through one entire sample paper until, two hours later, dot at one, the door bell rang again. It was Sonali again, this time, with a lunch box in her hand. Again she went straight to the kitchen, refusing my offer to help, and came out with two plates of food, one for me and one for herself. So, we were going to have lunch together! Overjoyed, I hurried to the dining table where she had laid the food out. It was a simple lunch of *daal, chawal, roti,* and *sabzi,* but eating it with Sonali made it special. We finished our lunch quickly, after which Sonali told me not to bother with the cleaning up. She would do it, she said. I went back to my room and studied for another hour before I got up and went to the kitchen to fetch myself a glass of water. I saw Sonali in the drawing room, sitting in the easy chair, a book held loosely in her hands, her eyes were closed. She appeared to have fallen asleep while reading. As she slept, the steady breeze of the ceiling fan kept making her hair fall softly over her face. Softly, I pushed her hair back away from her face and saw her expression relax immediately. But, soon enough, the fan did its job again and within a few minutes, the strands of hair I had pushed back were tickling her face again. Giving up, I just smiled and went back to my room. At around five, Sonali knocked on my room and came in with two cups of tea. We chitchatted for a while. I said nothing about having seen her sleeping. She left a little after half past five and told me to come over to her house for dinner.

"'It'll be a break for you as well, you've been studying all day,' she said.

"'True,' I nodded. And at eight in the evening, I joined her family for dinner. Her mother had prepared a special dinner for me to thank me for taking care of Sanket's studies. The day ended with me having added yet more moments to my kitty of memories. The next two days went by in a flurry of studying and going to the exam centre to sit for the exam. My *Chacha* and *Chachi* had been away from home for two days now and though I found it worrying, with Sonali's mother taking such good care of me, I did not let myself think too much about their absence, focussing all my energies, instead, on doing last minute revisions for the exams.

"I was walking out of the exam centre after the last paper, feeling relaxed and thinking about enjoying the rest of the summer, when destiny decided to give me a jolt and slap me out of my complacency.

"I was about to hail an auto to go back home, when I heard someone calling me. Turning around, I saw Sonali waiting for me on her Kinetic. Amazed, I hurried up to her.

"'Hey! What happened? How come you are here?' I asked.

"'Nothing has happened, Sunil, come, sit,' she said.

"I sat behind her on the Kinetic, but something about Sonali's unexpected arrival at the exam centre and her mysterious demeanour had unsettled me. My instincts told me that something was wrong somewhere. Immediately, I thought of my *Chacha* and *Chachi*. They had been away from home for two-three days now. Had something happened to them? I wanted to ask Sonali but since she was driving, I had to wait.

"Sonali took me to the old part of Lucknow, a place I had never visited before. She drove through narrow lanes, navigating expertly through the chaos and the rush. Finally, she stopped her Kinetic in the parking lot right outside the Balrampur Hospital, one of the most famous government hospitals in Lucknow. A hundred questions were burning inside me, but now, standing in the parking lot of the hospital, I knew something was very definitely wrong somewhere and I found myself too scared to say anything at all. Mutely, I followed her into the hospital. We crossed the reception area, the OPD, the recovery wards, and finally, Sonali stopped in front of the ICU. Before I could understand anything, Sharda, my younger sister had wrapped herself around me and was weeping even as my *Chacha ji* walked up to me, looking very tired and exhausted, and put an arm around my shoulder and walked me over to a line of empty chairs. My heart was thundering and with Sharda weeping on my shoulder, I knew it had to do with either my father or my mother. 'What happened?' I asked *Chacha ji* as I slumped into a chair.

"'It's your father, *beta*,' he replied softly, looking at me with great concern. 'But first, go and meet him. *Bhaiyya* has been asking for you . . . after that, I will tell you everything.' I nodded and went inside the ICU.

"My mother was sitting next to my father. She got up quietly when she saw me. Her eyes filled up with tears as she came and held me for a brief second before quickly leaving the room as only one person was allowed to sit next to the patient at a time. My father, I saw, was lying on the bed, fast asleep, his face slightly ashen, a drip attached to his left hand. Whatever it was that had landed him on the hospital bed, appeared to have shrunk him. He looked smaller and weaker, not like the strong, healthy man I had met the last time I had gone home, but a paler shadow of him. I just stood next to him, looking at him, unable to grasp just what was happening to me, to my family. He woke up after a while and smiled weakly on seeing me there. He beckoned me closer and I walked up to his bed and leaned in.

"'How was your exam, Sunil?' he asked. His voice was a whisper, a weak whisper that cost him much effort and left him exhausted.

"'It was fine, *Papa*,' I replied, not allowing myself to break down in front of him. 'Don't talk, *Papa*,' I said to him. 'Sleep for a little while longer, you need to conserve your strength to get better. I am going to go out and sit with, *Mummy*, okay? We'll be right here when you need us.'

"He nodded and closing his eyes tiredly, he drifted off to sleep again. I went out and sat next to my mother. 'What happened, *Mummy*? What happened to him?' I asked, my voice threatening to break.

"But instead of answering me, my mother started crying inconsolably. I tried to console her best I could, but with my own mind in a whirl, I was not able to do a good job of it. *Chachi ji* had come in while I had been with my father and she hurried forward now, sitting down next to my mother and holding her in her arms. *Chacha ji* gestured to me to walk out with him. Leaving my mother with *Chachi*, Sharda, and Sonali, I walked out of the hospital with *Chacha ji* and we went to one of tea shops outside the hospital gate. Ordering two cups of tea for us, my uncle sat down and told me everything that had transpired. 'Remember the storm that came about two nights before your first exam?' I nodded my head. 'Well, that storm hit Kalpi as well. In fact, it was even worse there. Lightening struck the main market and caused a short circuit which resulted in about fifteen-twenty shops getting completely gutted. Your father's shop was one of the ones burnt down. Not a single thing could be saved, Sunil, not a single thing. Your father has suffered a loss of at least twenty-twenty-five *lakhs*. And it is the shock of that loss that has landed him here at the hospital. We did not want to disturb you at this crucial juncture, *beta*. We knew it would have taken a toll on your exams. That's the reason we didn't tell you anything about all of this until now, and that's the reason why we all decided to stay here until your exams got over. Had your mother or Sharda gone back to my house to stay, you would have known that something was wrong . . .'

"*Chacha ji* trailed off, the exhaustion of the past few days was taking its toll on him. His eyes had dark circles under them and his face looked tired and pale. I looked at him and thanked God for giving my father such a wonderful brother, a brother who had put him before his own comfort and health. I took a deep breath and taking *Chacha ji's* hand in mine, I said, 'Thank you.' He looked up at me first in confusion and then, understanding the depth of my emotions, he gripped my hand hard, and nodded his head. I understood now that life never plays out the way we want it to, on the contrary, we are puppets in the hands of life and destiny. One might plan one's move, one might chart out the exact course one wants to follow, but just when things appear to fall into place, it is in God's nature to put us completely off course by throwing an unexpected challenge our way. And this was what my father's illness and the business loss was: a challenge that I had to face and overcome."

Chapter 14

"Life sure is unpredictable, huh?" Amit comments as Sunil breaks off.

"Yeah . . ." Sunil nods his head.

"What happened next?" Amit asked.

"Next . . . well, I sent my mother, Sharda, *Chacha, Chachi,* and Sonali back home and told them to get some rest while I stayed with my father at the hospital. My mother and *Chacha ji* came back later in the evening with my dinner and a small bag packed with things I would need for the night stay. After one more day in the ICU, my father was shifted back to the general ward where he was kept for two days to make sure that he did not suffer a relapse. After his release from hospital, we stayed in Lucknow for a week before leaving for Kalpi.

"Over the course of the next month, my father slowly regained his health under my mother's care and he started working towards getting his business back on its feet. The government gave only ten thousand rupees to all the shopkeepers who had lost their shops in the fire, irrespective of the actual extent of their financial losses. Most of the shopkeepers had no insurance to cover their losses either. A market generally runs on credit, and now began the daily hounding of the moneylenders. Like most other shopkeepers, my father too had taken credit to buy stock. Now, almost daily, we would find at least one of the moneylenders on our doorstep, making polite enquiries about my father's wellbeing, but actually looking for ways to get their money back. My mother sold some of her gold jewellery to pay off the moneylenders, but my father would need much more to restart his work. Finally, having no other option, my mother parted with some of the reserved gold she had been collecting for decades to use for Sharda's marriage, and along with the financial help my *Chacha ji* also extended, my father was able to start his work again on a small scale.

"I helped my father as much as I could. I accompanied him everywhere, be it to buy stock, or to the shop, or while finalising deals. I wondered, all along, what I should do next. Could I leave my father in this situation and pursue my own dreams? Could I go back to Lucknow or was I expected to stay in Kalpi? I longed to talk to Sonali. I missed her company. I had wanted to thank her and her family for helping me out so much during the crisis, but I hadn't found an opportunity to meet her before leaving. Now I wished I could talk to her and share my concerns and doubts with her.

"Two months went by like this until the day came when the result of my entrance exam was announced. I had gotten through HBTI, Kanpur. I was happy, no doubt, but at the same time, I was concerned about how my father would manage things if I left for Kanpur. Also, my studies would mean added expenses for him. My sister was also in the tenth standard, so there were her education expenses as well. Though we had managed to start our business on a small scale again, things were far from being stable. And I knew that my father, though he was not one to share his worries and anxieties, was worried about our futures. I had often found him sitting alone in the drawing room, his index finger twitching nervously as he fretted about how to manage things and earn enough money to support all of us.

"After a lot of hard thinking, I finally decided not to pursue engineering and help my father strengthen the business instead. After all, I reasoned with myself, I was anyway planning to take over the business from him eventually. Why not start now instead of waiting for years? When I informed my parents of my decision, my father got really upset. He did not want me to get into business, he said.

"'Look, business can be uncertain and unstable. A thunder storm can destroy your life's work and put you at the mercy of a moneylender, *beta*!' he exclaimed.

"But I stood firm with my decision. Finally, unable to make me change my mind, my father got *Chacha* and *Chachi* to come down to Kalpi and talk to me.

"'I know, I know, Sunil, that you want to stay here and help *bhaiyya*,' *Chacha ji* said even before I could say anything in my defence. 'But *beta*, you have worked hard for more than a year to get this seat. This is the fruit of your dedication and your labour. Do not give it up just like that.' He raised his hand and shut me up when I opened my mouth to protest. 'I know what you are thinking, Sunil,' he said. 'How will *Papa* pay for my education after the loss we have suffered? How will he manage all alone here? Well, let me tell you, Sunil, that your father is a strong man. He is capable of managing things in

Kalpi while you pursue your engineering. As for the expenses, I am happy to know that you are willing to sacrifice your future for the sake of your family, but really, you do not have to do anything of that sort. What I propose, *beta*, is this—that you accept my financial help in taking admission in Kanpur, after which you apply for a transfer to the Lucknow engineering college. I will help you get this transfer through my friends in the college administration. In fact, I have already spoken to them and they have assured me that this can be done very easily. You will continue to stay with us in order to cut down on living expenses, and you can take a couple of tuitions to earn some extra money while you study. That way, you won't be burdening your father with any financial demands at all. Now, do you agree that this solves all your problems?'

"I looked from my father to my *Chacha ji*. Both were beaming. Once again, my family had decided the course for my future, leaving me with nothing more than a nod of agreement to their plan. And so it was that I took admission in the engineering college in Kanpur and then promptly applied for a transfer to Lucknow.

"Settling back into Lucknow was not very difficult. Ajay had gotten admission in the engineering college in Jhansi and he had shifted while I had been in Kalpi. Such were the rigours of our college life that we found ourselves hardly in contact with each other. Sonali had taken admission in the BBA course at the Lucknow University, and since it fell on the way to my college, we started travelling together. I started taking tuitions for Sanket again, and this time, one of his friends also joined him. An extra student meant better money for me and I was happy that things were working out so well in this new phase. My father too appeared to be doing better with each passing day.

"My relationship with Sonali also deepened. We got to know each other much better as the time we spent with other lengthened. One day, I decided to invite her for lunch, but when I asked her, she refused. A little taken aback with her refusal, I decided not to push it since it could scare her off, but I couldn't help wondering about why she had refused me in the first place. A week later, while going to college, I asked her about it again. This time, she agreed.

"'I am free after two today,' she said. 'What about you?'

"'I'll manage something, don't worry,' I mumbled, trying to keep my excitement in check.

"Once in college, I realised I did not have sufficient money to go out for lunch with Sonali, so I asked one of my friends to help me out and with my wallet suitably loaded to foot the bill, I reached Sonali's college at around 1:50 p.m.. When she came out about ten minutes later, we decided to go to Hazratganj for lunch. Sonali said she wanted to have Chinese food, her weakness, at Jone Hing restaurant in Hazratganj. And all the way there, she sang great praises of the restaurant. It was easy to see that it was her favourite place.

"When we finally walked in through the doors of the Jone Hing restaurant, I immediately saw why she loved the place so much. Run by a Chinese family, the restaurant served authentic Chinese food at very affordable prices and was extremely popular with the city's food lovers. The ambience inside was also very appealing, with soft lighting and typically Chinese handicraft items decorating the walls.

"We settled into a corner table and made ourselves comfortable as a waiter came and served us water and gave us the menu card. We ordered vegetable fried rice with Manchurian and mutton chillies, Sonali's favourite dish, and within fifteen minutes, the food was on the table in front of us. The smell of the food was really appetising and both of us dug in with great enthusiasm. After taking a couple of bites of the mutton chillies, I looked up at Sonali and said, 'Can I ask you a question, Sonali?'

"'Yes you can!' she replied in between mouthfuls.

"'When I asked you a week ago to come with me for lunch, you said no, but today you agreed to my idea. Why so?'

"'Well I wanted to give you a party to celebrate your hard work and your success. But when you asked me a week back, I didn't have the money to treat you, but since now I do, I said yes to your lunch proposal. This is a treat from my side, all right? You can treat me some other time,' she quipped

"'All right, all right,' I nodded, smiling happily. 'Sonali, I want to share something with you, but I am not sure how you will react to it . . .'

"'Sunil, just go ahead and say it. You need not worry about my reactions. I know you have wanted to say something for a while now. Come on, say it, now I also want to hear it.'

"'Hmm . . .but before I do that, I want you to promise me that if you do not like it and are uncomfortable with what I am saying, you will tell me upfront to stop and that we will continue to be good friends even after that . . .'

"'Absolutely, Sunil.'

"Nodding, I took a deep breath and plunged straight ahead into what my heart had been wanting to say to her for a while now. 'Sonali, first I would like to thank you for all your support in all this time that I have known you. You might not realise it, but your words have been a constant inspiration for me and they have helped me in keeping my focus on shaping my future. I think that whatever I am today, at this moment, is because of your help and support. What you and your family did while I was facing the biggest crisis of my life so far is beyond a simple thank you. I am forever indebted to you and your family for all that you have done for us. I want to thank you, Sonali, for being in my life and for helping me shape it . . .'

"Sonali had been listening to me very patiently all this while, but when I trailed off, she started clapping. Taken aback, I looked at her questioningly, not able to gauge the expression on her face.

"'What are you doing?!' I asked, looking around furtively as other people in the restaurant turned to look at us. 'This is embarrassing! Stop it!' I protested.

"'What am I doing? Why, I am clapping. I mean, you just gave such a nice speech, you deserve an applause. I liked your speech, every word, every sentence, very nice, very nice . . .' she smirked.

"'Please Sonali, stop clapping.'

"She stopped clapping and stared at me. 'What do you think about me, Sunil? What kind of a person do you take me for? Do you really think I did what I did to hear you say all of this? To have your gratefulness in return? Really? She shook her head disappointedly. 'The day, I met you, Sunil, I saw you as a very balanced person. I felt that you might be the person who would be my best friend. I never expected that you to think like this . . . No, Sunil, I don't want your thank you and I don't want you gratefulness, okay?'

"'I am sorry, Sonali, I will not say something like this ever again, but yes, I am thankful to have you in my life and yes, you are my best friend too.'

"She nodded her head and began eating her food again.

"After a while, deciding I needed to lighten the atmosphere, I asked her, 'Do you know when was the first time I saw you?'

"'Umm . . . when you came to my house with Ajay *bhaiyya*?'

"'No, even before that!'

"'Really? When did you see me?' she asked, intrigued.

"I told her then the entire story of how I had first seen her by the chamfer that distant morning when I had been on my way to *doodhwala's* house. She laughed when the story was over. When the lunch ended a little while later, I knew in my heart that Sonali was nothing less than an answer to my prayers, she was the one who would soothe my broken heart and guide my soul to its purpose in this life.

Chapter 15

"How the time flies! It was the end of October 2002, *Diwali* was round the corner. I was in my fifth semester and Sonali was in her final year.

"Our past teaches us lessons which make us wiser in our present and our future. We learn to be more careful, more sensitive. Having suffered a broken heart once before, this time, with Sonali, I was extremely cautious and careful. Not once did I try to hurry things or force my feelings upon her. No, instead, I focussed all my energies on strengthening my bond with her. We went for movies together. We went exploring the city together, with her leading me around the older parts of Lucknow. We talked to each other for hours, discussing our plans for the future, our hopes and our dreams. There were so many things, so many small ways in which we shared ourselves with the other . . . With a million things going on in my life, it was good for me to have Sonali constantly by my side. She was not only an emotional support to me, what with everything that was going on with my family, but she also motivated me to concentrate on my studies and not get distracted by anything or anyone else. She was my closest, most treasured friend, an integral part of my life.

"I was supposed to go back home to Kalpi for *Diwali*, but before I left I wanted to take Sonali out somewhere to have a small, little pre-*Diwali* celebration with her. And I wanted no one else to be a part of this moment, except me and her. I wondered if I should gift her something as well, but I had never given her anything, no token of my love and my sentiments. However, when I got my tuition fee in advance, I decided to throw wind to my customary caution and planned not only a whole day's outing with her, but I also went to a jewellery shop and purchased a silver pendant, shaped like the letter S, for her. Of course to make myself feel a little better, I also bought a similar pendant for my sister Sharda and a few other things for my parents.

"Next day, I told Sonali about my plan of taking her to Kukrail, a famous picnic spot in Lucknow, and she agreed to it readily. We decided to make the trip on the 31st of October, a day before I were to leave for Kalpi.

"The day dawned clear and bright, the autumn sun feeling warm and soft as I waited for Sonali outside her house in the morning. The air had the slightest of nips to it, indicating that winter was but a month or so away. October and November have always been my favourite months, for there seems to be a certain magic in the air which lifts the heart and makes one want to just sit back and enjoy nature's glory.

"We had started for Kukrail quite early in the morning, and we reached there soon enough. Sonali had, of course, taken permission from her mother for coming along with me and her mother had agreed. Having known me for quite some time now, she trusted me enough to give permission to her daughter to spend the day with me. Sonali had warned me that there were not many good eating options inside the place, therefore, we had picked up some snacks and munchies en-route. We found ourselves a slightly shaded spot to sit in, the sun being still too strong and intense to be out in. I spent hours talking to her. And when I gave her the gift I had bought for her, she was thrilled. She had something for me as well, a red t-shirt. We'd been out for about four hours or so, when she suddenly started complaining of a severe headache. We'd already had our lunch by then, so I suggested we cut out trip short and head home. Probably being out for so long in the sun had caused her the headache, I reasoned.

"'You can buy a painkiller from some pharmacy on the way,' I suggested.

"To my surprise, however, she simply shook her head and took out an entire leaf of painkiller from her bag. 'I already have the medicine, Sunil!' she said, and taking the bottle of water from me, she quickly popped a pill into her mouth. As it turned out, she had been getting regular headaches for some time now which was why she had taken to carrying the painkiller with her at all times. Though I could see the colour returning to her face over the next few minutes, I told her go to a doctor and get the headache investigated.

"Next day, I left for Kalpi. It was good to be back home. My father looked better than before, though he was still not perfectly all right. Both my mother and my sister were ecstatic to see me. My mother hardly stepped out of the kitchen, so keen was she to feed her beloved son all his favourite dishes. They loved all the gifts I had bought for them. My sister was particularly thrilled with the locket I had purchased for her, and she wore it around her neck the minute I gave it to her. I met my school and *mohalla* friends in the evening a day after *Diwali*. But they were more eager to hear about the city I was living in and all the girls there than anything I really had to say, and their questions annoyed me.

"The next four-five days just flew by without my even being aware of the passage of time. Only when it was time for me to go back to Lucknow did I realise that my short *Diwali* holiday was over.

"On the eve of my departure, I was sitting in the kitchen in the evening while my mother prepared dinner for all of us, when, while talking to her about things, I found her little tense and anxious. Both my parents were not very fond of sharing their anxieties with us, but they had certain habits which gave them away. With my mother, her inner worry came out in the form of her rushing through whatever she would be doing at that time. Her movements and her words would become hurried and agitated, as if she couldn't wait to be done with them.

"I asked her what the matter was, but naturally, she was not ready to share anything with me. But I persisted in my questioning, and after about ten minutes or so, she broke down and started crying. Completely taken aback, I stared at her, aghast, unsure of what to do, how to console her, how to make her stop crying. I fetched a glass of water and forced her to drink a little from it. When she finally quieted, I asked her, very gently, to tell me, her son, what was causing her so much anxiety and tension. And only then did she reveal it all to me.

"'Sunil,' she said, her voice sounding tired and broken, 'you know that your father is working hard to re-establish his business, but how can years and years of labour and effort be replicated in months? Obviously, we have not reached the level where we can feel safe about our future financial expenses. We are able to manage our day to day expenses, but you know that Sharda is going to be eighteen next month and we need start preparing for her marriage over the next couple of years. A girl's marriage is always an expensive affair. And there is lot of dowry that's required in our caste. But with our current situation, when we are living a more-or-less hand to mouth existence, how can we afford to marry her off?

"'Your father, he never shares anything with me, never tells us of the hundred different worries that are eating him up from inside, but I know. I know how these fears and thoughts keep him awake at night. Why do you think his recovery is so slow? It because he keeps worrying . . . I regularly try and console him that everything will be all right, but how much good will my words do when all he does is smile back at me and never share what's going on his mind?' She wrung her hands helplessly and looked at me with pleading eyes, silently hoping I would be able to do something to ease the situation.

"But I did not really know what to say to her or what to do. She had told me so much in one go that I was still trying to wrap my head around it. Of course I hadn't been unaware of the financial trouble my family had been facing, but I had not realised the extent to which it was threatening our future happiness. I had never thought that one single thunderstorm could cast its shadow over the future of my sister. There was nothing really that I could have done, at least not immediately because I needed two more years to finish my education and start earning enough money to be able to support my parents and my sister. But until then, what? I knew that we could of course seek help from *Chacha ji*. But he had already helped my father out with some money with which to restart the business, and he himself was a salaried man with only so much income. Would it even be right to take help from him again?

"While I battled with these questions inside my head, my mother continued to look at me with hopeful eyes. I realised then the amount of hope a mother places in her son to make things all right. Her expectations were at once overwhelming and uplifting. I was determined to do my best for my parents, but, until I spoke to my father and got a proper picture of the state of our affairs, there was nothing much that I could do.

"'All right, *Mummy*, I will talk to *Papa*. Together we will try and come up with a plan for the future. But please, do not cry again like this. I don't want to see you cry, okay? I am here, and so is *Papa*. We'll take care of things . . .'

"My mother nodded her head and smiled weakly, her face tear-stained, her eyes looking at me like an expectant kid's when he looks at someone for an answer.

"I spent the rest of the evening up on the terrace, watching dusk fall and darkness cover everything in its wake. The stars came out one by one, little dots of twinkling light in a dark, inky black sky. There was peace and serenity in everything around me, yet my heart was obviously not still. A hundred questions were tearing me apart. How was I going to deal with the situation? I couldn't really leave for Lucknow without talking to my father and sorting things out at least a little bit. But then, what would I say to him? What advice, what help could I offer to him? What could I possibly do to ease his burden a little?

"My sister's voice interrupted my thoughts. I was being summoned for dinner.

"'Coming!' I shouted back and got up from where I had been sitting on the parapet. I'll have to talk to *Papa* after dinner, I decided as I made my way down the stairs. And so, once done with dinner, I followed my father into his study where he was just settling down to some ledger work. I went and sat near him. He looked up at me, smiled, and then promptly busied himself with the ledger. I saw that he was transferring entries from the old ledger to a new one, for every *Diwali* it was customary to start a new ledger.

"'What's the matter, *beta*?' he asked after a while without looking up from the row upon row of numbers he was scribbling down onto the new ledger.

"I took a deep steadying breath. 'Is everything fine, *Papa*?' I asked.

"He looked at me, appearing a little surprised by my question, and then closed the ledger.

"'I am fine, if that's what you are asking. But who said I am not fine? Just look at me, am I looking unwell?'

"I smiled. '*Papa*, I want that you should not only look well, but also feel well. And no one has to tell me anything, I can very well see for myself that something has been troubling you for some time now. Tell me, what's going on in your mind?'

"'Nothing, nothing!' he dismissed me.

"I tried, I really tried to get him to talk, but he just wouldn't budge. I kept asking him to tell me what was wrong and he kept refusing to answer to my questions. My mother walked in a little later with his customary glass of milk. One look at both of us and she knew that I had been trying to talk to my father, but without any success. I looked at her and shrugged helplessly. My father caught the movement and he understood that my mother must have already apprised me of as much of the situation as she herself was aware of. When he looked at her questioningly, she averted her eyes. It was only then that he decided to give up and sighing deeply, he looked at me and said, 'See Sunil, we do have a problem, yes, but I also know that you do not have any solutions right now, so there is really no point in discussing these things right now. I just want you to concentrate on your studies for now. You are a responsible young boy, *beta*, and I know you have been nothing but a caring, loving, and ideal son. I know you will always take good care of us when we grow old, and when the time comes, I will share everything with you, but now, now you must focus on your studies and do well to make us proud.'

"'When you know that I am your caring son, why don't you share your troubles with me right now? And I assure you that I am concentrating solely on my studies. You do not have to worry about that getting affected by whatever it is that you tell me.'

"My father looked at me long and hard, and then, taking a deep breath, he started talking. 'Okay . . . I know, Sunil *beta*, that I need not to worry about your future. You have always been mature and wise enough to take care of it and not squander away your time in useless activities. As for what is troubling me, it's the thought of Sharda's marriage. Do you know how much your *Chacha* spent on Anju's marriage? Well, he spent close to ten *lakhs*! How will I ever save up so much money over the next couple of years? Sharda will also want to go to college . . . she wants to do a BSc and I cannot tell her that she can't because her father does not have the money to afford her education. I do not think that I can manage to save more than two *lakh* in next two years. I had dreamt of marrying off Sharda lavishly. Looks like my dream will remain a dream . . .'

"My father's drooped shoulders and my mother's downcast face tugged at my heart. The entire problem was rooted in an ancient custom which should have been eradicated from our society ages ago, but which, unfortunately, had managed to tenaciously hang on to our social setup. Dowry. If only the word had never existed! Life would surely have been so much more simpler for the Indian families caught in its trap. If my father did not have to think about paying a hefty dowry to secure a good husband for my sister, he could have breathed easy, but here he was, worrying about it day and night, losing his sleep, endangering his health. Were marriages a financial transaction between a boy and girl's families? And the more qualified and successful the boy, the more dowry that was demanded for him. Then it struck me, where my father had a daughter for whom dowry would have to be paid, he also had a son who could command a dowry himself. And then I said something which I had never thought myself capable of thinking or saying.

"'I understand your problem, *Papa*, and I also know that you are right in thinking that I have no solution to this problem right now. I can't support you for the next two years. That said, let me say this clearly: I am against dowry. It is a social evil that needs to be rooted out as soon as possible, but that is my personal opinion and I cannot impose it on others. I cannot single-handedly uproot a custom which has been going on for centuries now. But let us first look for a family who believes in discontinuing with the dowry system like we do, a family who will want their son to marry Sharda for who she is, a family that will not ask for dowry. I will help you in this search. Should we fail, then know this, I will suspend all my beliefs about the evilness of the dowry system and I will stand as your blank cheque. You can demand whatever amount you deem fit as a dowry from whomever you want to marry me off to. I will not say a word, all right?'

"My father said nothing to me. We were all silent for a long time afterwards, each lost in their own thoughts. When he finally got up to go to bed, he just put his hand on my head and nodded his head before walking out of the room. My mother, I saw, bent her head to hide her tears and wipe them away with the ends of her *sari's aanchal.*

"I had offered myself to my father as a means to an end, but how this would affect my life and my dream of forging a future with Sonali was something I just could not imagine.

Chapter 16

"Once back in Lucknow, I found myself consciously maintaining a distance from Sonali. Uncertainty about my own future meant that I could not allow myself to get any more involved with her. I limited my interactions with her. I tried to avoid her as much as possible and stopped discussing things about my life with her. Needless to say, Sonali was surprised with the drastic change in my behaviour, and though she tried to ask me if something was wrong, I dismissed her question every single time until she finally gave up asking me about it at all.

"A month after my return from Kalpi, my college department organised a day-long picnic trip to a place called Indira Aqueduct. Truth be told, with so much going on inside my head, I was not at all interested in spending an entire day with the people of my class, but spending an entire day all by myself, with no class, no college, no people to distract me meant even more hours battling the questions and the problems running inside my head. Therefore, in order to escape my own self, I decided to tag along for the picnic.

"A day before the picnic, I met Sonali on my way back from college. We chitchatted for a couple of minutes, and I casually mentioned that she'd have to travel to and fro to her college alone the next day since I would be gone for the college picnic. She nodded her head, told me to have fun at the picnic, and then left. The next day, I left home early and made my way to the Nishatganj crossing, the designated pickup point for all of us. It was around half-past ten in morning when we finally reached the picnic spot. The stuffy bus ride and all the highway dust had not dampened the spirits of my classmates, and it was with much cheering and singing that they all got off the bus one after the other. As it turned out, Indira Aqueduct was a picnic spot much in demand. The parking lot where our bus dropped us was quite full with school buses and other private vehicles.

"We walked into the park, a total of about forty-five to fifty students and some faculty members, and looked around for a place to set base in. It was just the beginning of winter and the sun's warmth had started mellowing a little bit. After we found ourselves a good space under a tree, we were divided into smaller groups of about six students each with a teacher at the head and left to explore the area. Built over the river Gomti, Indira Aqueduct is quite an engineering feat by itself and it attracts a lot of people every day who come and marvel over it. When we saw the structure, we were all amazed at the capacity of the human mind to invent and design such things as will make lives better. We spent a good amount of time exploring the entire area and enjoying the winter sun before deciding to head back to where we had set base.

"It was when we came back after our exploration of the site that my world started to tremble and shake a little. A small group of eight-nine girls had settled themselves quite near to where we had all kept our stuff. There were about two men—they looked like the daily wage labourers employed by the Aqueduct administration for the daily upkeep of the place—who were helping them settle down. Some of the boys from my class were, quite expectantly, making catcalls in the girls' direction. I sauntered over to where the boys were standing and looked closely at the girls and I almost had my eyes popping right out of my head when I saw Sonali amongst the girls. What in the world was she doing there? Completely stunned, I stared at her as she, oblivious to my eyes on her, went about settling down with her friends. Why was she there? Had she already made a plan with her friends before I had told her about my college picnic yesterday? Or had she made her plan after coming to know about my plan? But how did she manage to plan things so quickly and at such a short notice then? Was her being there a co-incidence? Or was she there for me? My heart was thundering loudly inside my chest and I was still trying to understand what exactly was going on when we got summoned back to our resting area for refreshments. Sonali had still not seen me, and I decided to sit behind the tree while I ate the *samosa* and the *soanpapdi* that had been packed for us. I didn't want her to spot me, not just yet. I thought more about her presence at the Aqueduct as I ate, but I was unable to come to any conclusion. My heart kept telling me that she was here for me, that she wanted to tell me something, but what was it that she could possibly be trying to tell me was beyond my understanding.

"It was when my classmates decided to play *antakshari* after the meal that Sonali finally looked in my direction and saw me. I had been watching her all this while and therefore I saw the first moment when she spotted me. There was no surprise on her face at seeing me there. She just smiled in my direction. The percentage of boys in my class far outweighed the percentage of girls and therefore, when the entire class was divided into boys versus girls for the *antakshari*, some of the girls from my class went and approached Sonali's group and asked them to join their team for the game. They accepted the offer and Sonali and her friends moved up to where we all were sitting and presently the game was underway. We played till around four in the afternoon, and throughout, both Sonali and me kept stealing glances at each other, taking care that no one caught us doing so. And just before we all left, Sonali came up to me and told me to meet her a little later at Jone Hing in Hazratganj. My heart, quite naturally, did a quick somersault, before settling back to its thunderous beating.

"It took me about an hour and a half to reach Hazratganj. When I entered the restaurant Sonali had called me, I found that there was no one there except for her. I walked up to the nicely secluded corner table that she had occupied and slipped into the seat across from here. Without saying a word, she beckoned the waiter and placed a quick order of mutton chillies, noodles, and some cold drink. Unsure and slightly nervous, I looked everywhere around the restaurant, but not at her. I could feel her eyes boring into me. 'Are you all right, Sunil?' she finally broke the uncomfortable silence that had crept up around us.

"'Ugh . . . yes, I am fine,' I replied, slightly surprised with her question.

"'Are you sure?'

"'Yes, of course I am sure,' I insisted, beginning to become a little apprehensive about the strange direction the conversation appeared to be taking. 'But why are you asking this question?' I enquired hesitantly a heartbeat later.

"'Well, ever since you came back from home, you seem to be going out of your way to avoid me, to spend less and less time with me. You don't talk to me properly and even when you do, it's mostly monosyllabic answers to questions I ask. It appears to me that you seem to be hiding something from me. There is something going on in your mind and your heart which you are keeping from me and this feeling is really pinching me. Please share your troubles with me, Sunil . . . tell me what's the matter. I want to know what has happened which has made you so distant from me.'

"I stared at Sonali, clueless as to what to tell her, how to best answer her without provoking further questions from her. She had hit the nail on its head and landed me in a fix. I had somehow never thought that she would be so well attuned to my moods that she would guess that something had happened back in Kalpi which had greatly affected me. Granted that she was a very good friend, someone I thought I was falling in love with, but what had transpired in Kalpi, what I promised to my worried parents back home was something too personal and too big to be shared with someone who was still technically only a friend.

"'Nothing, Sonali,' I hastened to assure her, 'I am not hiding anything. Trust me.'

"Sonali continued staring at me. She didn't say a word, but her penetrating gaze pinned me to my chair and made me squirm uncomfortably. Suddenly, I felt like I was a nursery school student who was being grilled by his headmistress for some mischief he had done. 'Really, Sonali, trust me, I am not hiding anything.' I tried to get away again, but she would have none of it. She could see through my lie, I realised. I felt like a bird trapped in a net, the more I tried to free myself, the more entangled and caught I became.

"'Sunil?' My name on her lips fell like a soft, gentle drop of soothing water, a balm to my frazzled nerves, and finally, I gave in to my urge to unburden myself and told her about everything that had happened in Kalpi.

"Sonali didn't utter a single word as I talked. She heard everything patiently, her face not giving away even an iota of what she was thinking. The waiter came and served us our food, but neither she nor I touched it. The steam rising from the mutton chillies filled the air around us with an aroma which would have made us jump at the food on any other day, but when I looked at her and gestured towards the food, she shook her head and said she wasn't hungry anymore and asked me to continue with my story. The food grew cold, and the moisture droplets condensing on the two glasses of cold drinks on the table seeped into the tablecloth, dampening it, but I continued pouring my heart out. I left nothing out, and when I was finally done with my story, she continued sitting silently as she had all this while. She didn't stir. She didn't say a word. Nothing. 'Say something, Sonali . . .' I finally pleaded after an unbearably long moment of silence.

"'How serious you are about your commitment to your father?'

"'I don't know . . .' I swallowed, 'I really don't know . . . all I can say is that I do not want them distressed over anything.'

"'I can understand your problem, I can . . . but did you even stop once to think about me? With what you promised your father, did you think about what will happen to me now?'

"Stunned, confused, and a little scared, I stared at her. What did she mean by asking me what would happen to her now? Did it mean what I thought it meant? Should I ask her to repeat herself? Did I hear her words right? Was what I heard exactly the same as what she actually said, or was there a difference between the two? 'What are you saying, Sonali?' I blundered ahead, 'I-I-I didn't get it. What do you mean?'

"Instead of answering me, Sonali bowed her head and sat stock still, only her shoulders moving up and down as she drew in deep breathes. A moment later, a drop of water fell on the table cloth in front of her. It was only then that I realised that Sonali was crying. Terrified now, I reached across the table and gently nudged her hand, but she didn't react. I understood vaguely, the full import of what she had been trying to tell me, but I wanted to hear the words again for that my mind could believe them and memorise them. Oh, God can you please help me here? I sent a silent prayer towards the heavens above. Can you please send me back a few seconds so that I can relive and cherish this moment for which I have been waiting since forever now? But of course, there is no time machine that exists to send us back into our pasts. We can only forge ahead into our futures and so I did, saying the first thing that came to my mind, ''e, ahem, Sonali . . . err . . . we are good friends, Sonali—"

"'Good friends?!' Sonali exclaimed, looking up at me with anger beginning to spark in her tear-filled eyes.

"'I-I-I err—'

"'No, Sunil, enough!' she cut me short. 'We have come a long way, Sunil, and we have been through many ups and downs together. We have shared our dreams and our desires with each other, and you say we are 'GOOD FRIENDS'?'

"Sonali's voice had gone up to a dangerous level. I looked around nervously. Thankfully, there were still no other customers in the restaurant, but the serving staff had begun hovering in the background, eager for more spicy snippets of this apparent quarrel between two young people.

"'I thought, Sunil, that we were beyond the confines of a simple friendship, that there is something deeper, something more worthwhile to our relationship, but it appears to me that I have been wrong all along. Tell me, do you really only consider me as your friend?'

"Life sometimes puts you at such a crossroad that there is no going back. I regretted having unburdened myself in front of her. I regretted having promised my parents to be their blank cheque, but at each of these points in my life, I had no other option but to do what I did. I looked at Sonali sitting in front of me, her heart out in her hands for me, her eyes shining with unshed tears, her face so troubled . . . and I knew that where I had given her the absolute truth a moment ago, my love for her, and her love for me deserved a chance, and thus did I manage to save myself from losing her in entirety in that moment.

"'I am not in a position to make any promises, Sonali, but give me a little time, and I will do everything that I can to resolve this situation . . . and no, you are not just a 'friend' to me, you are more, much more . . .'

Chapter 17

"'Dil bhi ek zid pe ada hain,
Kisi bacche ki tarah,
Ya to isse sab kuch hi chaahiye,
Ya kuch bhi nahin.'

"These words from one of Jagjit Singh's *ghazals* were my constant companion over the next couple of months.

"While my daily life continued the way it had been before, the emotional upheaval caused by my last conversation with Sonali had caused a storm of emotions in my heart. I had no immediate solution at hand to offer to Sonali. The only thing I could do was waiting for time to take its course. My tuition classes with Sanket and his friend had continued uninterrupted all this while. I went to Sonali's house every day, but I never saw her. Sanket told me that she hadn't been keeping well of late, but afraid that I was the culprit of her ill health, I never asked to meet her and never made detailed enquiries about the reason for her repeatedly falling sick. Fear and guilt can make great fools out of us, blinding us from the realities of life and allowing us to live in our own little worlds.

"One day, when I reached Sonali's house for the daily tuition class, no one opened the door to my persistent ringing of the doorbell. I walked around the house and checked the backdoor, but that too was locked. I walked back to the front door and rang the bell again. Nothing. I waited for a minute and then put my ear to the door. At first I heard nothing, but then I heard the distinct sound of feet shuffling towards the door. I stepped back and the next instant the door was opened. It was Sonali. But she looked terrible. She was dressed in a pair of old *pyjamas* and a loose tee shirt, both crumpled and looking slept-in. Her face looked pale and tired. There were dark circles under her eyes. Her hair hung about her face in tangles, limp and not combed. She was looking really really sick, nothing like the person I had always known—smiling, cheerful, carefully and neatly dressed, a spark of happiness always present in her very being. I was shocked, to say the least.

"'Ahem,' I cleared my throat. 'Is Sanket at home?'

"'No, his football team has a final match in the RDSO ground. My parents have taken him there,' she replied, looking at me with a terribly blank expression on her face.

"'Oh, ok,' I nodded my head dumbly, not knowing what else to say. Something about her stony look and her unwelcoming stance was making me very uncomfortable. She hadn't asked me in yet, and given that there was no one in the house, I thought it prudent to leave. But somehow I couldn't. I couldn't get over the Sonali standing in front of me. How different was she from the girl I had known all this while. A part of me blamed me for her condition, but then the other part wondered why she hadn't believed me when I had said that I needed some time to sort things out.

"'What happened to you? Are you all right?' I blurted out, more to drown out the questions inside my head than to continue this stilted conversation with her.

"Instead of replying, however, Sonali simply turned around and walked back inside the house, leaving the door behind her wide open. I was left standing there, by the main door, not knowing whether I was to follow her in or just leave. A minute later, I walked into the house and found her sitting on a sofa in the drawing, her head held in her hands. I went and sat down next to her. She didn't look up even once, not when she heard me walk in, and not when she must have surely felt the sofa shift under my weight as I sat down.

"'Sonali,' I spoke gently this time, 'are you all right? What has happened to you?'

"She looked at me finally. 'Does it really matter to you, Sunil?' she asked, her voice sounding broken.

"'It does, Sonali. Of course it matters to me. I would never want to see you like this . . . looking so unwell, so weak. I am not sure what picture you have painted of me in your mind, but I am not that bad a person. It is just that time and circumstances are not in my favour right now. I told you that I cannot promise anything, not right now, not when nothing is under my control, but I also said I would try. I know that it is only a matter of time before I am in a position from where I can work everything out in my favour. I have never done anyone any wrong in my entire life, I have never thought ill of someone, never boded ill will, my karma is clean, and that, I believe, will make things come around, that will bring us back together. I want most to be able to do justice to my family, to my future, and to you, Sonali. To you. I know you love me. I knew it for sure that day when you laid bare the pain in your heart over what had happened in Kalpi, but did you ever think that I love you just as much?'

"I felt her go still next to me. She was waiting for my next words with bated breath. Picking up her hand and holding it gently in mine, I continued, 'Since the first time I saw you, my heart has not been in my control, not even for a minute. All it does it think about you. Every hour, every day, every month, all this while, you are always in my thoughts. You are my thought. You are in my dreams, in my hopes, in my aspirations. Whenever I wake up in the morning, I want see you the first thing. Whenever I talk to you, I feel confident about myself, I get motivated. Whenever I am in trouble, you always have a solution. Whenever I have something to celebrate, who do I want to celebrate it with? You. It is only your name that always comes to my mind. If I say I do not love you, I will be cheating myself more than anyone else.'

"I brought her hand up to my lips and kissed it before continuing with what I had to say, 'The truth is, Sonali, that in spite of our love for each other, you will have to give me some time, may be a year or two, to decide what can be done to take care of things. We should work together on trying to figure out a solution to get me out of this crisis situation.'

"Exhausted of all words to make her believe me again, I stopped, looking at her with pleading eyes. But instead of saying something, Sonali withdrew her hand from mine, stood up, and walked away towards her room. I tried to stop her, but she didn't heed a word and just walked into her room and locked it from inside. I knocked on the door and begged her to open it but she didn't. I could hear her crying on the other side and in vain I tried to console her with meaningless words, but nothing worked. She kept crying and telling me to leave her alone, and the more I tried to talk to her, the louder her sobs became. I did not want to leave her like that, but seeing that my being there only made her feel more miserable, I left with a silent good bye.

"Life moved on at its own pace over the next couple of months. I finished my sixth semester exams and along with Ajay, who was in Lucknow for a short while before seventh semester started, I joined Java classes as that would give us an added advantage while looking for jobs later. My tuition classes at Sonali's house continued as before, but neither did I meet her, nor did Sanket tell me anything about her. Increasingly, I sensed a rather strained atmosphere at her house, but not wanting to intrude, I never tried to find out anything about it. Many times I thought of calling Sonali on her telephone, but each time, I stopped, for what could I possibly say to her? Being without the only true friend I'd ever had, the one person I loved so much, was terrible. My life, I thought, had hit rock bottom.

"But life, as we all know it, has some cruel aces up its sleeves.

"It was just another day sometime in the month of March and when I woke up in the morning, Sonali's silence a now familiar weight tugging at the bottom of my heart, I had no clue, no clue at all, about just what the day held in store for me. Ignorant as I was of all that fate was lining up against me, I went about my day as usual, brushing my teeth, having *chai* with my *Chachi* and *Chacha*, quickly scanning through the newspaper, getting ready for college . . . devoting my time and all my energies into maintaining the rhythm of all those small activities that make up the daily grind of our lives, those tiny little moments that work together to maintain balance and keep the machinery of our life rolling along just fine. Fool that I was, how was I to know that all hell would break loose in the evening after my tuition class with Sanket got over.

"'All right then, that's it for today. Finish this maths exercise by tomorrow so that I can continue the lesson forward,' I said to Sanket, closing the mathematics text book and getting up to gather my things and leave.

"'Umm . . . *Bhaiyya*,' Sanket interrupted me, '*Papa* asked me to tell you to meet him before you leave.'

"'Oh, okay! Sure thing, I will see him on my way out.' I wondered what possibly Sanket's father wanted from me. Had Sonali told him about everything? No, no, I reassured myself, he probably wanted a simple update about Sanket's progress with the studies. Feeling a little less nervous, I walked over to the drawing and found him there, sitting with a half-empty cup of tea in his hand. He seemed preoccupied with something and he didn't hear me enter the room. I waited a moment before I pointedly cleared my throat, trying to grab his attention.

"'Ahem . . . *Namaste* Uncle!'

"He started on hearing my voice. 'Oh, Sunil Come come, *beta*. I was waiting for you only. Come have a seat.' He beckoned me in and I walked over and sat down in front of him . . . the rest of that evening, however, is still an absolute blur in my memory, Amit . . ." Sunil shudders.

Years have passed between then and now, but though he does not remember the words that Sonali's father used to tell him what was happening, the overwhelming panic and the engulfing pain of those moments is as fresh in his heart as a wound newly acquired. Every time he thinks back to those moments, all he can think is just how fragile life is at all times, how it takes less than a fraction of a second to completely shatter someone's world, to upset things, to break someone's heart, to inflict pain. Sunil takes a long sip of his drink before continuing with his story.

"I couldn't understand a word of what Sonali's father was saying to me that day, it was just all random words that made no sense, it was all just noise. I wanted to run from there, but respect and politeness demanded that I stay there in that room which had begun to stifle me until he finished talking. And the minute he fell silent, I got up and ran. I didn't look back. I didn't bother to wish him a polite good evening before I left. No. I just threw open the main door and ran out, taking in deep gulps of the fresh air outside as if my lungs had been starved of all the oxygen they required to breathe and keep me alive.

"I walked back home in a daze, not able to process what I had been told. I ate dinner, I slept, I woke up the next morning, went to market for something my *chachi* has asked, went to the Java class in the evening, again attending to the mundane details of my life like a robot. That entire day passed thus, with me suspended in this weird state of disbelief and denial. My thoughts were still incoherent, my ability to put everything together still weak. It was the day after, that I found myself processing things and it only happened because Ajay noticed my distracted state during the evening Java class and cornered me after class and persisted in me telling him what was bothering me until I did exactly that. I told him what Sonali's father had told me—that Sonali had some critical illness which was still undergoing investigation, that the doctors were still trying to reach a diagnosis, that she was not responding to medical treatment as well as she should have, that things were beginning to look very very grim, and that the worse could happen any time. Sonali, my beloved Sonali, was battling death, and it was a losing battle.

Chapter 18

"My conversation with Ajay that distant evening made it clear to me that while I had always tried to be fair with my parents—putting them and their welfare before everything else, keeping my own dreams aside to fulfil my responsibilities towards them, going to the extent of controlling my emotions and my love even after it became clear to me that Sonali was just as much in love with me as I was in love with her—it was now my responsibility to show my love and support towards Sonali. Ajay pointed out, very correctly, that Sonali had supported me when my father had fallen sick just before my entrance exam. She had stood right next to me and helped me right through those difficult times. Not once had she hesitated to help me in whichever way she could. She had been true to our friendship, to our affection for each other. Now, with her facing perhaps the biggest and toughest fight of her life, wasn't it not only fair, but also essential that I stand by her side as well? If not for the sake of our tender love, I owed it to our years of friendship to be with her.

"Next day, determined to do what was right in my opinion, I decided to begin trying to make Sonali talk to me again. Right after breakfast, I quickly showered and changed and walked right over to her house, stopping on the way to purchase a bouquet of pink roses for her. When I rang the doorbell, it was her mother who opened the door, and seeing me there, she smiled and ushered me right in. Her parents had been well aware of how deep our friendship was, and our recent distance must have been noticed by them. Her mother looked at me with great understanding, knowing that her husband had informed me of Sonali's condition only a couple of days before. Without a word she led me to Sonali's room and left me at the door, silently gesturing that I was to go in.

"Tragedies and moments of misfortune create great waves of empathy between humans which makes them do things which they normally would never have done. I knew that under normal circumstances I would never have been allowed to enter Sonali's room alone. The rules of social propriety would never have allowed for such transgressions, but Sonali's mother probably understood that I needed to make amends, that I needed to do my bit in helping Sonali face this cruel twist in her fate.

"I knocked on the door. Perhaps she had never expected it to be me knocking on her door again, or perhaps she thought it was her brother, not me, who was knocking on her door, but that same cruel fate which had landed her in this battle in the first place, made her say 'Come in' in response to my knocking. And thus, I won myself a chance to be with Sonali all over again. She was reading a novel when I walked in, lying on her stomach on her bed, her chin resting on two pillows under her face, a thick fat book in her hands. Her hair fell partly over her face, shielding it from my view.

"'What is? What do you want, Sanket?' she asked, not bothering to look up from her book.

"So she had mistaken my knock for Sanket's. I quietly walked up to the bed and pulling a chair alongside it, I sat down. At the sound of the chair being pulled, she turned her head and looked back, and seeing me, she sat up straight. The shock and the surprise on her face told me enough about how she must have given up hope on ever renewing our relationship again. My heart pained a little, thinking how little she must have trusted me to do what would hopefully be good for both of us. I took a deep breath and forced myself to stop thinking like that, and then, garnering courage, I smiled and gave her the flowers. She hesitated for about a minute before taking the flowers from my outstretched hands. She didn't say anything. Neither a 'thank you' nor a 'what are you doing here?' She buried her nose into the bouquet, taking deep long breathes, as if to memorise the smell of these flowers, these pink roses that I had bought for her because I knew they were her favourite flowers. Is this what a terminal illness does to you? I wondered silently. Does everything become something that needs to be memorised so that you can remember what you life was like before it got swept away in a sea storm of medicines, tests, hospital visits, doctors in long white coats, doctors with grim faces? Did the ordinary parts of daily life become bigger and much more lovelier with the prospect of death becoming more real and more daunting than what it is for those of us who calmly believe it to be only something which comes when one is old and weak and frail enough? Sonali's face had a pinched look to it. And the dullness and the tiredness I had sensed in her being the last time I had seen her was even more pronounced now. How fast am I losing her? I asked myself, feeling a little scared all over again. All through the previous night, the thought of ever having to be without Sonali had kept me awake. Life without her around would be like a gaping, threatening void which nothing and no one could ever fill. I sat up straighter, mentally shaking my head over my own morbid thoughts. I was there to help and take care of Sonali, to show her my love. I wasn't there to sit and meditate about death and the fatality of human life.

"'How are you now?' I asked her.

"'I am all right . . .' Sonali replied, her voice neutral, her face half hidden behind the pink roses.

"'Sonali, I have been wanting to talk to you for quite some time now . . . I wanted to say something to you, but I never managed to gather the courage to do so before today . . .' I trailed off, peering at her in order to gauge her reaction. But her face gave nothing away and I decided to carry on anyway.

"'Ever since our last discussion, Sonali, I have spent hours thinking about everything. About my family, my life, about you . . . There was confusion in my heart, a tug of war, with my responsibility towards my parents pulling against the desires of my heart. I felt my soul getting torn between the two. Believe me when I tell you that it was hellish. The questions haunted me, day and night, each day, every day. I haven't been able to sleep. I haven't been able to study. I go through the motions of everyday life like a mindless robot, doing one thing after the other, fulfilling the role that I am expected to play out in the drama of life, but my mind and my heart, they are always with you, Sonali. They have always always been only with you.

"'I have taken a lot of time, I know, perhaps I have taken more time than was necessary, but Sonali, now that I am sitting here before you, what I have to say next is something that I have full belief in. My words come straight from my heart . . . there is no deceit, no lies, no scope for any misunderstanding anywhere now. I have cleared away all my doubts and questions and Sonali, this here is what I have to say to you now . . . this is my admission of love:

"'My heart beats for you and you alone. I want to be with you every day, through all the hours that the ticking clock gives us in a day. I want to be with you for as long as God grants us the gift of love. I told you once before that you are all that I long for, all that I want in my life. To be with you, to see you, to hear you talk, laugh, sing, to see you smile, to look into your eyes . . . that is what I want. But I know how cruel life can be. I know how different responsibilities can force themselves upon you and make you give them top priority amongst everything else. But that is the way of life, Sonali. Devoting ourselves to accomplishing things and fulfilling the various roles and responsibilities that are given to us is a part of living. Never does it mean that you yourself have become less important to me. Never will it ever mean that I care less for you and your happiness . . . no Sonali.

"'My mistake until now has been that I thought it impossible to balance responsibility with love. I did not think it possible that I could do my duty towards my parents and still manage to accomplish my heart's deepest desire—to be with you, now, forever, and always. As long as you agree to stay by my side, be my partner in everything that life throws our way, there is nothing I cannot do. You are the reason for everything that I am today, Sonali. You give me hope. You give me courage. You give me love. You are everything to me, Sonali. I love you. I have always loved you. And I will always always love you . . .'

"Exhausted, I leaned back into the chair and closed my eyes for a brief second. My heart felt lighter, yet at the same time, I was scared. I had laid my soul bare in front of Sonali in the hope that she would forgive me and give me a chance to give her the love she truly deserved. I did not want to imagine a scenario where she would reject me and everything I had said and ask me to leave her alone forever.

"I opened my eyes slowly, a little hesitantly. But when I saw the look on Sonali's face, I knew at once that God had been merciful. He had not denied me a chance to make things better. Her eyes were moist and before I knew what was happening, she had both her hands around my neck and was weeping softly. I held her like that for a couple of minutes, letting her cry all her pain and her grief out before we spoke of our feelings. It took her a while to calm down, but when she did, I gently wiped her cheeks dry of the tears and shifted to the bed, sitting right next to her. She leaned into me, resting her head on my shoulder as I held her.

"It had taken us close to four years to reach a place where we could tell the other of the great love that we had always felt for them. But it was a wait worth every day of those four years. Sitting there like that, with her next to me, my arm around her slim waist, her head resting on my shoulder, the air around us scented with the smell of the roses I had brought for her, it was all so bittersweet, so peaceful. My rioting heart stilled and I bent down to place a soft kiss on her forehead, pouring all my pent up love and affection into that simple, chaste action. And that was how my love story with Sonali finally started . . .

Chapter 19

"Sonali's response to the treatment being given to her was very slow. But still, at least she was responding and that alone was a big thing for all of us. There were numerous tests that were performed on her in order to properly diagnose the reason for her condition. And when the results all came in, we were all shocked. Sonali was diagnosed with a brain tumour, somewhere between a Stage II and a Stage III. Doctors advised surgery to remove the tumour, but in her current condition, Sonali was deemed unfit for surgery. Not only was she bodily weak and vulnerable, but mentally too, she was not strong enough to motivate herself to pull through the post-operation phase of recovery.

"'She needs to strengthen her will to come out of this illness,' her father said to me a few days after the results came in. He had stopped me after my tuition class with Sanket ended and was bringing me up to date with the doctors' prognosis of Sonali's condition. 'The doctors have suggested September for the surgery,' he continued. 'It's a good time because she would be done with her BBA by then and she'll have time to take the compulsory two-month bedrest after the surgery.'

"'Hmm . . .' I nodded my head. The news about Sonali's tumour had stunned me, and though it had been a couple of days since we all found out about it, having a definite name for the illness that was slowly claiming Sonali made it much more real and much more harder to bear. But I knew Sonali's father was right. She did not appear to have a strong will to fight the illness and recover from it. She seemed to be wilting away a little by little every day, right in front of us. Then and there I resolved to infuse Sonali with hope and a desire to get better. Ever since my confession of love to her, things had changed dramatically between us, and both me and Sonali had started to spend more and more time with each other. Every evening, for instance, after my tuition class, I would take Sonali out for a short walk around the park near her house. The tumour had left her so weak that she could not walk for more than twenty minutes, but even those twenty minutes with her were extremely special.

"We all continued thus for a little while, all of us trying to strengthen Sonali in order to make her fit for surgery.

"The next wave that hit my life and shook it up happened on an innocuous Sunday. Sonali's parents were going to Kanpur to attend a family function and because they could obviously not take Sonali along, it was decided that Sanket would stay back. However, just to be more assured about things, they asked me to stay at their house until they returned later in the evening.

"Come Sunday, I reached Sonali's place early in the morning right as her parents were leaving. Once they left, we first had some breakfast and then sat chatting and talking in the drawing room, with the television on in the background, until lunchtime. Sonali's mother had prepared a simple light lunch for us and we quickly finished it all up. After lunch, Sanket went to play with his friends, while I insisted that Sonali go take a nap.

"I was sitting in the drawing room and going through the newspaper when someone snatched it from my hands from behind. Surprised, I turned around and saw that it was Sonali, now standing with the paper held behind her back, a mischievous grin on her face, and her eyes teasing.

"'What are you doing here?' I demanded, trying hard to sound stern and angry. 'I just told you to go and take some rest!'

"'I couldn't fall asleep!' she replied, still grinning.

"I tried to stare her down into giving me the newspaper, but when she didn't, suddenly, I lunged towards her and tried to snatch it back. Sonali, however, was much faster than I had anticipated and she nimbly sidestepped me. Every time I tried to take the newspaper from her, she ran away from me. I tried my level best, chasing her around the drawing room for some time but finally I gave up. I was tired and so I sat down on the sofa and she came and sat down next to me. I looked at her and saw that she was still grinning. I had been afraid that all the running around would have tired her, but the glimmer of excitement in her eyes told me that she more happy than tired. But there was something else there as well, something that told me that Sonali wanted to say something to me but was hesitating.

"'What is it?' I asked. 'Why are you looking at me like that? Is there something you want to say to me?'

"'Sunil,' she sighed deeply, bowing her head a little dejectedly, 'you know that I need to undergo surgery . . . but I am not sure whether I will survive the operation or not. I am really frightened . . .' she looked up at me, her eyes filling up with tears. The fear that she felt was clearly visible on her face. 'I know the doctors want me to be mentally prepared for this surgery, but I do not want to die. And my heart says that I will not live through the surgery . . . I will not get better . . . and with each passing day . . .' she trailed off, unable to go on. I held her hand in mine, squeezing it gently, hoping to impart some of my love into her through the gesture. I couldn't bear to hear her talk like this. I didn't want her to think about dying, no, not when she was so young, so beautiful. Taking a deep, shuddering breath, Sonali began speaking again. 'With each passing day, Sunil, I find myself coming closer to you. My thoughts are always with you and about you. All I want now is to live. Live with you. Together. Please Sunil, please save me. I want to be with you forever!'

"What can you possibly tell a girl who is fighting a terminal illness? What could I possibly say to this beautiful girl sitting in front of me asking me to save her? I felt helpless, like never before. I wanted to reach up through the skies and shake God into agreeing to take all of this away. I wished all of this were an ugly nightmare. That I should wake up the next instant and find the world a lovely, rosy place to live in . . . with Sonali waiting for me at the far end, her arms wide open, her face bathed in a smile, her eyes shining with love. But no, all of that was never to be. I had to fight back my anger over God and be strong. I had to be strong for Sonali.

"Saying nothing, I brought her hand up to my lips and kissed it before leaning over and kissing her on her forehead.

Pulling a little away, I looked at her and smiled. 'I am always always going to be with you, my dear,' I spoke gently, my voice not more than a loving whisper for I wanted my words to tell her how deep my love for her went. 'I know you are scared, but this surgery is important for you and you know that. It is the only way we can beat this illness and start a future together. If you insist on behaving like a child, how will you gather the inner strength that's required for you this battle?'

"'But I don't want to die. I know the doctors will not be able to save me. I know it!' she started sounding like a sulky, petulant child.

"'How can you say that with such a confidence, Sonali? Doctors are considered right next to God. Their hands have the gift of life . . . man has trusted his life to a doctor for centuries now, then why do you mistrust them like this? Why are you so tensed? Nothing will happen to you. Trust me. I am here with you. Your entire family is with you. And we'll all be with you all the way. And where is your faith in God? God throws us tough challenges, he tests us, but he is never cruel. He will definitely hear our prayers and make you better.'

"'Doctors cannot save me now, I am beyond medical help, I know it,' she insisted.

"Seeing that she was beginning to get increasingly agitated, I decided to let it go. Instead of trying to convince her, I asked her, 'All right, relax, calm down. So tell me, what do you want to do?'

"'I want to live my dream before I die,' she replied instantly, as if all along, she'd had these words ready in her heart. 'And my dream is to stay with you. Not forever, I mean I know I won't live forever . . . but I want to stay with you for as long as

I have time left. All my remaining days I want to spend with you . . . your studies are getting over. And once you find a job, we can get married. You will leave for office in the morning and I'll take care of our house after you leave. I'll cook, I'll clean, I'll do everything. In the evening, I will wait for you to come home. I would have already cooked dinner by then, it would be your favourite dishes that I cook every day. When I hear you opening the door, I will hide myself somewhere in house. You will look for me in the entire house and then suddenly, I will come up on you from behind and close your eyes. You will act like you are surprised. You will pretend that you do not know who I am. You will beg and plead with me to let you go, but I won't budge. Finally, you will try and bribe me with something and eager to see what you are bribing me with, I will remove my hands from your eyes. You will open your eyes and see me, and happy to be back home, you will pull me to you and hug me.' Sonali looked up at me with a great smile on her face. Her eyes were glowing with a dreamy look that told me that she must have imagined this entire scene many times by now.

"'Amen!' I said, my heart breaking a little at the apparent innocence of Sonali's dreams. 'I pray that whatever you just said, comes true for us one day . . . But for now, you have to stop thinking about all these things. Your every wish will get fulfilled, my dear, but you need to just give some time to things . . . you need to think positive. You needn't think of us as a dream. You and I living together, in a house of our own, everything will become a reality in the time to come. And I promise to do everything that I can do to make it all real, to change your dreams into reality. All I want you to do is focus on getting well. Once you are all right, once we've emerged victorious, we will begin our life together. I promise . . .'

"Sonali smiled weakly, but half a second later, her face acquired a downcast look again.

"'What happened?' I asked.

"'I don't want to think about anything else apart from fulfilling my dream. I don't want to focus on anything else, not my surgery, not my illness, not anything else. I want at least one of my dreams to be fulfilled right away and only then will I consider everything you asked me to do . . .'

"What dream could she possibly want fulfilled right away? I wondered. She was looking at me peculiarly, as if everything depended on what I would say next.

"'May I ask you something right now, Sunil?' she broke in, making me snap out of my thoughts.

"I stared at Sonali, unable to react, wondering what she could possibly want from me right now. She took my silence as my concurrence and without any further dilly-dallying, she said, 'Will you marry me right now?'

"There are certain moments in life when the world comes to a stop and time stands still. The only way you can tell that this has happened is because blood drums in your ears for a second before this happens, it drums loud and hard and thunderous, filling your head with sound. It makes you think of ocean waves crashing all around you, and then, just as suddenly as it had begun, it stops. Everything stills. There is no sound, no movement, and no activity anywhere around you. And so I sat there, right next to Sonali, stunned, stilled, and shocked by her words. My thoughts were all haywire, my emotions all jumbled up. My mind told me to tell her that what she'd said was ridiculous. We couldn't just get married like this. But my heart told me to wait and not rush into saying something I couldn't take back. It told me to take a deep breath and then, then when I felt my nerves beginning to calm down a little, my heart whispered that I couldn't break Sonali's heart. No matter what I really felt or wanted, I could not hurt her. And then, was it not exactly this that I wanted? To be with the love of my life for as long as possible?

"'Yes,' I said suddenly, surprising my own self. 'Yes we can get married. But how we can do it right now?'

"Perhaps she had never expected that I would agree to her request so easily and quickly because she looked stunned, as if she could not quite believe what she had just heard. But when I continued to look into her eyes steadily, she stood up and gestured to me to follow her. I got up and reached for her hand, and with our hands held tight, she led me to the small altar her mother had created in one corner of the dining room. There, she unfolded a prayer mat and spreading it out on the floor in front of the altar, she sat down on her knees.

"'Come sit,' she said. 'Let's talk to God.'

"I followed her example and sat down, my hands folded in front of me and my eyes closed. I felt her take a long deep breath next to me and then she began:

"'God, you know everything. If there is someone in this world I love more than anything or anyone else, it is Sunil. I want to live and die with him, God, but my time, I know, is limited. I know I will never be able to actually live to see the day when we can get married properly, when we set up our own home, have children, bring them up . . . all those dreams need a lifetime . . . Today, in front of you, I want to accept Sunil as my husband, in heart, soul, and mind. We want to marry in front of you, for you alone are fully aware of the depth of our feelings, you alone know that this is what my heart desires the most . . . We need someone as a witness for this marriage and you are our witness. You are our only witness. No one will ever know about this marriage, but knowing that you know will be enough for us. We have nothing to hide from you, God. Our love is deep and pure and we seek your blessings . . .'

"I felt my heart about to explode. A great love for Sonali was coursing through my veins. I kept my eyes closed even after she had finished. I wanted to let God know that I loved her, that I would do whatever it took to make her happy, that I agreed with every word that she'd said.

"I felt her getting up beside me. And then, she kissed me on my forehead before walking away. I opened my eyes and saw her walking towards her room. I followed her into her room. She went and sat down on her bed, patting the space next to her for me to come and sit on. I went and sat next to her. We sat quietly for a long moment, and then, I turned around and put my hands around her face to force her to turn towards me. And then, looking deep into her eyes, I said, 'I love you, Sonali, and I can never live without you . . .'

"Sonali said nothing. She just smiled, a smile of such great peace and joy that I can still feel it warm my heart. I leaned forward and rested my head against her forehead, breathing deeply into her smell. She closed her eyes. I could see that her breathing had become a little ragged, a little fast. My own heart was jumping around inside my chest like an excited little child. Up close, I could see how soft and delicate her skin was, like a pearl. She had the longest eyelashes, mesmerising, alluring. And her lips, they were like two perfect petals of a delicate flower. I sucked my breath. Oh God she was beautiful!

The next moment, before I could fully assess what I was doing, I kissed her. It was a kiss of great longing, of immense love, of two hearts thundering and beating as one. Waves of happiness flowed through me, making me feel light headed. It was like a moment caught on a slow motion film in a camera. I felt everything clearly, deeply, and acutely—her soft lips against mine, our eyes closed, all sensations new and exciting, my skin prickling with intoxication, my heart beating harder, faster. It was a warm sea of beautiful emotions that was sloshing around inside my head. And all of this happened within a fraction of a second before I realised that I was actually kissing her. When the realisation struck, I thought I should pull back, but I couldn't, because Sonali choose that very instant to respond to my kiss. She pulled me closer and kissed me back with as much passion and as much love as I had poured into my kiss. The flame of our love leapt high. It was as if I had touched a live wire. My nerves tingled and adrenaline coursed through my body, making me want more, making me forget all boundaries. But I reigned myself in. I forced myself to pull back.

"I opened my eyes and looked at her, passion making her blush, her eyes heavy with all the desires she held inside her heart. I held her still within my arms. We were struggling to catch our breaths.

"'I love you . . .' she whispered a moment later.

"'And I love you too. . .'

Chapter 20

"It was the beginning of September. The date fixed for Sonali's surgery approached quickly. A day before the operation, she was admitted to PGI, one of the super-specialty hospitals in Lucknow, for all the preliminary tests and examinations. Sanket had been sent to stay with one of his friend for next few days because Sonali's parents were going to stay in the hospital for the first couple of days before and after the surgery. I accompanied Sonali, her parents, and Sanket to the hospital in the morning and stayed there the entire day. In the evening, Sanket and I left. We would be back very early the next morning to see Sonali before she was taken for the surgery.

"When I said goodbye to her that evening, I wanted to tell her once again that I loved her, but with so many people around, it was obviously not possible. I could see that she was a little scared and I wanted to hold her in my arms and reassure her that everything would be all right, but all I could do was stick to my correct, formal mannerism and politely bid Sonali and her parents good night and leave.

"That night, the hours ticked by with my mind building up pictures of a beautiful future ahead with Sonali, as if it wanted to tease me. How would she look in a *sari*? Does she know how to cook? Will she want to stay at home and take care of things on the domestic front or would she want to work after we got properly married? Where we would go for our holidays? It was an endless list of such seemingly mundane questions that ran round and round inside my head. While my heart beat with trepidation over what lay ahead, my mind conjured up pictures of the future. It was a restless sleep that I finally fell into and when the alarm shrilly woke me up in the morning, it had only been a couple of hours of sleep that I had managed.

"I got ready quickly, still a little groggy, still feeling the lack of sleep burn my eyes. My *Chachi* knew about the operation and she had woken up much before me and prepared lunch for Sonali's family and me and packed it all into a big tiffin, kept ready on the dining table.

"'Sunil, have *chai* before you leave . . .' she called me.

"I went into the kitchen and silently had the hot tea she put in front of me. I didn't talk, I couldn't find anything to say, and knowing how worried I was, *Chachi* did not try to force me into a conversation. Just as I was leaving, she stopped me and said, 'Everything will be all right, *beta*, Keep faith on God.'

"Smiling weakly, I nodded and left.

"One small good thing was that Ajay was in Lucknow. Some brawl in his college had gotten out of hand and had resulted in the college being shut down for about two odd weeks. A couple of days earlier, I had told him about the operation and had asked him to accompany me to the hospital on the day of surgery itself. He had, of course, readily agreed.

"I made my way over to Ajay's house and found him already waiting at the gate. I nodded at him in greeting, and without wasting time on exchanging pleasantries, we started on our bicycles. Now, PGI lies quite outside the main city itself, on the Rai Bareli road, and reaching there is no mean feat. We had only reached Charbagh, which lay midway, when we realised that cycling all the way to the hospital had not only been a stupid idea because it was tiring us out, but it would also make us reach the hospital late and that would mean that I wouldn't get to see Sonali before they took her to the OT.

"'Let's park our cycles at the railway station parking lot and take a bus to the hospital, huh?' Ajay suggested, pointing to the railway station which thankfully lay just ahead of us. I nodded in agreement and we quickly parked our bicycles at railway station and came out to wait for a bus at the bus stand right near the station. Within ten minutes, we got onto a bus and were on our way to PGI.

"When we finally reached the hospital, Sonali was more-or-less ready to go to the operation theatre. Her parents were hovering over her, and it was difficult for me to say anything to her. She was dressed in a light green hospital gown that reached up to her knees and her hair had been removed and she was wearing a shower cap of sorts to keep it all in place. Seated in a wheelchair, ready to be wheeled into the OT, she looked small and vulnerable. If only I could pick her up in my arms and whisk her somewhere far away from this nightmare. We looked at each other and I tried to silently convey to her the emotions that were raging in my heart. Finally, they came, a nurse and an intern, and they took her away to the OT, allowing us only to accompany her till the swinging doors of the room, and there, just before she disappeared from our sights, Sonali turned around and smiled at us. A smile of love, of bravery, of courage, and of hope. And then she was gone.

"The hours ticked by slowly. One long minute after the other. My head and my heart were devoid of any thought and any emotion as morning became noon and noon became afternoon. It was a long operation, we had all known that, but nothing had prepared us for the agony that it is to wait for hours and hours to be told whether the person you loved, the person getting operated on the other side of that door, was alive or not.

"It was close to half past five in the evening when the doctor supervising Sonali's operation came out of the OT with a reassuring smile on his face.

"'The operation went off fine,' he said the minute we spotted him. 'The next forty-eight hours, however, are extremely crucial and we will be keeping Sonali under very strict observation in the ICU.'

"We all sagged with relief and sent silent prayers of thanks. A little later, after making sure that Sonali's parents ate dinner, Sanket, Ajay, and I left, promising to be back in the morning the next day.

"There was nothing much to do the next day, though both Sanket and me were there at the hospital quite early. Sonali was obviously still in the ICU and no one was allowed to visit her. We had been told by the nursing staff that she was doing all right and would be shifted back to her room the next morning. I insisted that Sonali's parents go back home for some rest while Sanket and me stayed in the hospital until they returned for the night. They agreed and once they left, the rest of the day passed by in trying to ward off boredom while sitting inside a hospital room. There was still an air of unreality to the proceedings inside my head. I couldn't believe it was all actually happening. But it was, and it was only the next day, when I saw Sonali after she had been shifted to her private room, that the reality sank in.

"She lay on the bed, awake, but only mildly so, the painkillers and the strong medication she was on making her drowsy, causing her to drift in and out of consciousness. Her head was covered in bandages, a thick padding of white hospital gauze that half-hid her face. Her left hand had piercings in a couple of places as the nurses had not been able to find a vein for the IV drip on first try itself.

"*Tup-tup-tup* . . . the liquid medicine in the IV drip dripped its way into her veins. Her parents had gone home for a while, leaving me and Sanket to keep an eye on things. Sanket had gone to the hospital pharmacy to buy some of the drugs the doctor had prescribed, and I had been left alone with Sonali in the room. Those rare minutes were precious to me and I picked up her right hand in mine. It was limp and cold, and lay in my hands a little lifelessly. With the affect of the anaesthesia wearing off, the pain that she was going through was clearly visible on Sonali's face. Looking at her I wanted to throttle someone for all the unfairness that was so typical of life. What gave God the right to make good, honest people suffer like this?

"I wanted to do something to ease her pain, but I knew that there was nothing I could do. I was stroking her hand gently when she opened her eyes and looked at me. She tried to smile but she couldn't do more than give me a brave watery half-smile. Her eyes bore into mine and I sensed that she wanted me to say something to her, anything that could distract her from the pain. As if soft words could be the medicine for unbearable pain.

"'Sonali, my brave love, you have no idea how beautiful a sight your smile is to me right now! Oh the agonising hours I have spent longing to see this smile of yours! Your operation was successful . . . God has been kind to us, Sonali. I know you are in a lot of pain, but much as I want to take it all away from you, I can do nothing but sit here and watch you suffer. I cannot share your pain, my dear, but I can feel it. Be brave, braver than what you already are. You have to fight your way out of this pain and regain your health for my sake, for the sake of your parents, for the sake of our future together . . . You know, if I were in your place right now, I would have broken down by now, but not you. You are one of the God's brave angels who was sent to this world to teach me to live, love, and be kind and generous. You are my lucky star, my dear, you are my luck star . . .'

Chapter 21

"A week after the surgery, Sonali was discharged from the hospital and allowed to go home. The doctor gave her parents a long strict list of things she could and could not do. She was advised complete rest for the next two months and everything from her diet to her physical activities were under supervision. Every day, after the tuition class, I would go and meet her and spend some time with her. She did not like being forced to stay inside, but she was still weak and vulnerable. Often she would be irritated with being cooped up inside, then I would try to cheer her up by telling her about things that had happened during the day, or regaling her with funny stories and jokes.

"The first time she was allowed to step out after the surgery, I took her to the Tikait Rai pond which wasn't very far from our colony. She had been excited all day at the prospect of going out and while we set out with great enthusiasm, she tired out much sooner than either of us had anticipated, and within an hour, I brought her back home. But it had been a good outing, for her spirits at least, and her recovery after that was better and slightly faster.

"In the January of the next year, campus recruitment started in my college and I put my heart and soul into preparing for the exhaustive rounds of interviews with companies that were being put together for us. I had already spoken to Sonali about this, and we had decided that for a week before the interview, I should only focus on preparing myself. Therefore, I cut short my daily visits to Sonali's house and spent all my time studying and preparing myself. In the end, after many many rounds of interviews and group discussion, all my hard work paid off and I got placed in Tata Consultancy Services with a starting salary of twenty-five thousand a month. I would have to go for a six-months training course in Gurgaon and only after that would I get my first proper posting in one of the many TCS offices scattered across the country.

"To say that it was a big day in my life when I got that call letter, would be an understatement. The day I got the letter from TCS was probably the biggest, happiest, and most fantastic day of my life. In those moments when I held the letter in my hand and read the words printed on it, it felt as if the world shifted a little and everything, every single thing that had ever been wrong with it fell right back into place. Everything that I had wanted and dreamt of was there in my life—the girl I loved had survived a life-threatening surgery and was well on the road to recovery, and I had landed a very good job with a prestigious firm, a job that would not only allow me to fulfil my duties towards my parents and my sister, but a job that would also give me the opportunity to actually go about realising my dream with Sonali. God had tested me in numerous ways over the years, but now finally, things seemed to be happening just the way I wanted them to.

"It was with a spring in my step that I went home that day after college. When I reached home, the first thing I did was to give my *Chachi* the call letter and touch her feet, for it was truly her blessings and her generous taking care of me that had enabled me to come this far. *Chacha ji* was ecstatic when he heard the news in the evening and later, around dinner time when I knew my father would be back home from the shop, I called them and told them the good news. There was a lot of happiness all around and my mother, overwhelmed with the good fortune, almost burst out into tears.

"I couldn't meet Sonali that very day, but the next day, come evening, I went over to her house and, with her mother's permission, took her a nearby park where we could sit and talk peacefully. Any other time and I would have probably taken her out for a nice dinner somewhere and then given her my piece of good news, but she was still not allowed to go out too much and eating out in a restaurant was definitely not an option.

"Tikait Rai pond had become quite a favourite with Sonali over the past few months and that was where I took her. We sat on a bench by the edge of the pond, watching the sun begin to go down in the distant horizon, painting the sky a beautiful gold and red as it went down

"'I have some good news for us,' I said after a while.

"Sonali turned and looked at me. "Tell me?" she said, eager like a small child waiting for a lollipop.

"'I got my first job offer letter!' I exclaimed, unable to contain myself anymore.

"Sonali stared at me, stunned, speechless, her eyes going even wider when I pulled out the TCS envelope from my jacket pocket and handed it to her. She opened it and read it, word by word, not once but twice, and then, when she finally looked up from the letter, I saw the happiness mirrored clearly on her face.

"'Oh Sunil!' she whispered, finding herself unable to say anything more, her eyes wet with what I correctly presumed to be tears of joy.

"'You know Sonali, I have been waiting for this moment for years now. I have had only two wishes in my life till now—one was to have you with me always, and the other was to get a good, well-paying job after completing my graduation. Today, both my wishes have finally come true. You came into my life like an angel, Sonali, and you changed the way I looked at life. You made sure that even in the hardest and bleakest of times, I had a positive outlook towards life. You made me realise that life is God's finest gift to man and that it is our responsibility to enjoy it thoroughly and do justice to it . . .'

"I looked at her expectantly, and though she was smiling and nodding her head, I sensed immediately that there was something going on in her mind that she was not telling me.

"'What happened, Sonali? What's the matter? Are you not happy?' I asked, a little taken aback by her silence and the peculiar expression on her face.

"'No, no, Sunil. I am very happy . . .' she trailed off.

"Something about her entire demeanour and her voice alerted me to the fact that there was something she was definitely not telling me. Come to think of it, ever since I had picked her up from her house in the evening, there had been a strange hesitation, a weird negativity around her, as if she was afraid of something. I had been so eager to share my news with her and see her expression on hearing it that I had not paid much heed to any of it.

"'Come on Sonali, it's me, your Sunil, I can tell when you are hiding something from me . . .'

"She shuddered a little, but said nothing. Inching closer, I took her hands in mine. They were ice cold. Rubbing them gently between my hands, I nudged her, 'Tell me, Sonali, what is it?'

"'Sunil, I am happy that you got such a good job, believe me, I would never want anything but the very best for you . . . but Sunil, I have now become very superstitious of late. I do not know why it is so, but with each passing day I feel more and more convinced that I will not be with you forever. And the more I think about it, the more I become possessive and fearful! And now, if you go away to Gurgaon for six months . . . I don't know Sunil. What if I never see you again?!'

"'But why are you becoming so negative?' I asked. 'We have only just reached a point from where we can actually achieve all those things which we dreamt about! Everything is going so well. Your operation was successful. Your recovery has been good, and it is just a matter of another few weeks before you'll be able to resume most of your daily activities like before. When everyone around you is beginning to be so positive about things, why are you yourself so downcast and so negative?!'

"'I do not know, Sunil. But my sixth sense says that what we want in our lives, is not what we get. I feel like I am fighting for my dream against my destiny. The more I think about you, the more I get frightened about the future. I am not a coward, but I feel that God is not going to give me a long enough life to be with you forever . . .'

"Sonali's words were beginning to worry me. Before her illness, she had been one of the most positive people I had ever known, but now, hearing her talk like this, I felt a little nervous. 'Why are you thinking like this? God is with us and our prayers will make sure that nothing ever happens to you.' I smiled, trying to put on a brave face for her benefit. 'You are my brave girl and I want you to be always brave, okay? So stop thinking about everything else and focus only on living in the moment and enjoying yourself. As for my job, it is a happy achievement which could not have happened had you not supported me all through this time.'

"She smiled and nodded.

"'Come, let us imagine that the world is going to come to an end tomorrow and there will be no one left alive the day after . . . we have only today to live and everything that we want to do has to be done today. Forget your worries, Sonali and treat each day as if it were the last day before a coming apocalypse . . .'

"Sonali sighed and kept her head on my shoulder and we sat on that park bench for a little while longer as the evening fog descended and wrapped itself around us. And when it started becoming a little chilly, I took my love back home.

Chapter 22

"It's easy to get lulled into a sense of everything being all right because the mind seeks ways of ignoring all those things that might puncture its bubble. We allow ourselves to believe that our lives and our worlds are invincible, that nothing bad or unwanted can happen to us, but the truth is, the next challenge in our lives is always waiting for us just round the corner.

"With my final semester exams approaching, I began gearing up in earnest for this last lap of my studies. While I was looking forward to the next phase of my life, there was also a sense of nostalgia over the world I was going to leave behind. I knew that once I stepped out in the real adult world of job, offices, salaries etc, there would be no childlike innocence left. There was a hectic round of visiting all the favourite haunts on the college campus and meeting the favourite teachers before we all left for our preparatory leave. My exams went off quite well and it was with a sense of great relief that I walked out of the exam hall after the last paper. We had a couple of weeks off before we all left to join our places of work. Most of my classmates had great plans of either travelling to nice places with their friends or partying every night, but I was still contemplating whether to spend all this time with my parents in Kalpi or to stay in Lucknow and spend the holidays with Sonali.

"That same evening, after coming back home from the exam and having rested for a while, I freshened up and walked over to Sonali's house. Her father was at home when I reached and he ushered me into the drawing, gesturing me to sit. He called out to his wife and told her to make two cups of tea for us and then sat down on the sofa in front of me.

"'How was your exam, Sunil? Went well, I hope?'

"'Yes, Uncle, it went well . . . I put in my best. Let's hope the results are good.'

"'Hmm . . . so what is your plan now? Sonali told us about your getting a job with TCS. That is wonderful news, *beta*. We are very happy for you.'

"'Thank you, Uncle. It is only the blessings of my elders that has brought me so far . . .'

"'When will you be joining? Your training is in Gurgaon, right?'

"'Yes. I was thinking I'll split my time between here and home, as in spend a few days at each place before going to Gurgaon for the training.'

"Uncle nodded his head thoughtfully. He then removed his spectacles and putting them on the table next to him, he rubbed the bridge of his nose absent-mindedly. I peered at him and noticed for the first time that he looked a little tired and worried. I was about to ask if something was wrong, when he looked up at and said, 'Sunil, I have some bad news . . . Sonali has been complaining of a headache for a couple of days. She hid it from us for about a week before her mother managed to coax it out of her while oiling her hair. She says she didn't want to worry us by telling us about the headache. Anyway, I took her for a check-up immediately. The doctors did a few scans and ran a couple of tests and things don't look so good. They have asked us to get a biopsy done, but Sonali, well, she refused to get the test done without you by her side.'

"I had been sitting stunned, but I looked up sharply at that. Why had Sonali made her affection for me so evident to her parents? I wondered.

"'It's all right, Sunil,' her father said, understanding my confusion. 'We understand your feelings . . .'

"I nodded, my throat feeling tight. 'But why didn't you tell me about this immediately?' I asked after a moment, sounding a little impatient at this delay.

"'Well, since your exams were going on, Sonali insisted that we wait for them to get over. She did not want to disturb you . . .' he replied simply.

"Typically Sonali, I thought to myself. I could not believe what I was hearing. I could feel anger surge through me. I wanted to break something, hit somebody, and do something to release all the anger. But I couldn't. Instead, I had to allow it to choke me while I sat in front of Sonali's father. Now, at the back of my mind, I could understand Sonali's irrational her fear about not having enough time. She must have just started getting those headaches again that time and she must have naturally realised that her recovery was not progressing as it should have. Oh God, please let everything be all right! I prayed desperately. 'Have you taken the appointment or do we still need to take it?' I asked Uncle.

"'No no, I have already taken the appointment for day after because they'll need a day to do some pre-tests . . .'

"'And the results will take approximately a week to come in, right?' I asked.

"'Yes,' he nodded.

"Sonali's mother entered the room just then with a tray with two cups of tea and some refreshments. She smiled at me a little tiredly. It was clear to see that her daughter's health was weighing heavily on her mind. She kept the tray on the table in front of us and left without a word.

"'I have two weeks of holidays before I leave for Gurgaon,' I said, picking up a cup of tea and taking a slow sip. 'If I stay here for ten days and then go home to be with my parents for about five days, do you think that will work?'

"'Yes yes,' Uncle replied, 'I think that should be fine as we will have all the necessary reports by then.'

"'Hmm . . .' we lapsed into a silence after that, the only sound in the room being that of us intermittently sipping the tea. Once done, I took leave from Sonali's father and walked into the kitchen to seek her mother's permission to meet her.

"'Of course, Sunil,' her mother replied when I asked if I could see Sonali. 'She is in her room. Go meet her and see if you can cheer her up a little . . .'

"I opened the door to Sonali's room quietly, and without knocking on the door, I walked in. She was sitting on a rocking chair by the window with her back towards the door and appeared to be reading a book. Taking a deep breath I forced myself to smile—I didn't want her to see my disturbed expressions—and quietly crept up on her, closing her eyes from behind when I was directly behind her. Where I expected her to squeal in surprise and try guessing who it was and demand to be released immediately, she did no such thing. Calmly putting the book on her lap, she touched my hands once, and said, 'Sunil, how are you?'

"Surprised, I walked around the chair and sat on the bed next to her. 'This is not fair!' I exclaimed. 'How did you know it was me?! I walked in so quietly.' Shrugging, she just smiled. 'Anyway, how are you feeling now?'

"'I am better now as you are with me,' she teased. 'How was your exam?' she asked seriously a second later.

"'It was good . . . but let's how the actual results are . . .'

"'Your results will be excellent, Sunil, don't worry,' she assured me. 'You worked really hard, my dear, and all that hard work will definitely pay off. I am very happy, Sunil. Things are finally looking up for you.'

"'But I am not all that happy, Sonali. I cannot bear the thought of having to go far away from you and that too now. Why do we not have any good IT companies in Lucknow so that I can work and still be near you?' I literally wailed. 'I don't want to go to Gurgaon . . . and you have started hiding things from everyone and when I will not be here, then there will be no around with whom you can share stuff . . .'

"'No, Sunil, don't worry please . . . I promise I will not hide anything from anyone from now onwards . . .' she fell silent. 'I guess *Papa* has already told you about the biopsy?' I nodded my head in response. She continued, 'Well . . . I am scared, I admit, it's like my fear about not having a long enough life to spend with you is coming true . . . but Sunil, *Mummy* spoke to me a couple of days back . . . we had a long chat and she told me that both she and *Papa* like you a lot and they are hoping that we both can eventually get married and live our lives together . . . now that I have their blessings, I don't want to die, Sunil. I want to live now!'

"'Oh Sonali!' I got up from the bed and knelt in front of her and gathered her in my arms. In spite of everything that was happening, it was a relief to hear Sonali say that she wanted to live.

"The next two days were spent in getting a flurry of tests done and then, we had to wait an entire week before we could find out about Sonali's fate. That week was a nightmare, everyone trying to be brave, but the fear of death haunting everyone's nights and making sleep extremely hard to come by. I went to a nearby temple to take God's blessings and pleaded with him to keep Sonali safe and strong.

"When the day of collecting the test results came, I went with her father to pick up the reports and from there, we went to the hospital where we had an appointment with the doctor to discuss the results with him. On reaching the hospital, however, we were told that the doctor had been caught up in an emergency surgery and would take some time. With no other option but to wait, we sat down in the reception lobby and waited for the doctor to be free. We were there for almost an hour, each minute inching by like an hour. Finally, when the doctor was free to see us, we were directed to his cabin. He took the reports from us and studied them minutely for a long time before he looked up at us.

"'How is Sonali?' he asked Sonali's father.

"'She is fine . . .' Uncle responded.

"'Is she keeping happy?'

"'Yes, she is. But why are you asking such things? Why don't you tell us whether she is fine or not?'

"The doctor kept the report on the table and said, 'The reports are not in her favour. I was suspicious of something being wrong when Sonali began complaining of having a headache again . . . and now my suspicions have been confirmed. Sonali has metastatic brain tumour and it has spread through her brain and also infected her lungs. It is rare, such a relapse, and happens to only in one in a million cases. I am very sorry to tell you this, but the chances of her survival are very low. At the max, I can say that she will live for about six more months . . .'

"We sat in stupefied silence in front of the doctor, our mouths hanging open, our faces blank. Seeing that we were both unable to react, the doctor continued, 'But miracles happen all the time . . . they have happened in the past and they will continue to happen in future. It all depends on how much willpower she shows in fighting against the illness . . . but we cannot do anything for her now . . . I am sorry.'

"I couldn't believe I was hearing the right words. Was she really dying? My Sonali?

"'D-d-doctor," Uncle stammered, 'I, ahem, I err . . . I u-u-u- understand what you are saying . . . but can you please tell me how many such c-c-c-ca-cases of a patient beating this illness have actually h-h-h-ha-happened in past?'

"'There are many cases of survival, but not in this category. But yes, people do live longer than what we anticipate. You cannot hope for what it clearly inevitably, but you can hope that she will live for a little longer than what I have just predicted . . . you all should try and make her as happy as possible. Make her feel loved . . . that is all that you can do.'

"We walked out of the doctor's chamber without a word. Uncle called from the hospital to Aunty and since I was standing right next to him I overheard his side of the conversation.

"'*Hello? Yes it's me . . . yes we met him. He said she is fine. Ask Sanket to bring some sweets and see if you can make something special for dinner tonight. We should celebrate this good news, and yes, Sunil will also join us.*'

"I was looking at him peculiarly when he turned around to face me after disconnecting the phone. He shrugged helpless before explaining himself to me.

"'I just couldn't make myself tell her everything that the doctor told us . . . see Sunil, I stay out of the house most of the time for work and it is easy for me to hide my emotions. But Sonali's mother . . . she stays at home and will be with her for most of the time. If I tell her what the doctor told us, then it will be really really difficult for her to pretend that everything is all right, especially around Sonali. Being a mother, she may not be able to hide her emotions. That's why I think that it really makes sense that we should hide all of this from her and Sanket.'

"I agreed with Uncle's rationale. 'Uncle,' I spoke up a minute later, 'I am thinking that perhaps I should turn down the TCS offer. I don't want to leave for Gurgaon at this time. I want to be here with Sonali for as long as she needs me around . . . and it's not like there are no jobs in Lucknow . . . am sure if I look around I will find a good job for myself.'

"'No Sunil!' Uncle spoke sharply. 'I cannot allow you to jeopardise your career like this. You have been there for Sonali more than we could have ever expected from you . . . you have been a big source of support to me as well. But now you must think about your career. You will not turn down the TCS offer. How would you explain that to Sonali? Did you think about that? She will only become suspicious if you turn down such a good opportunity.

"'Sunil, I suggest that you go and meet your parents for a couple of days and then come back and spend the rest of your holiday with Sonali . . . as for when you do leave for Gurgaon, well, both you and Sonali can get mobile phones and keep talking to each other regularly, all right?'

"I nodded, seeing the sense in Uncle's words.

"A day after that, I went home to Kalpi for two days and then, what remained of my break, I spent with Sonali, creating precious memories and dreams that would fill my heart with equal parts happiness and equal parts sadness later.

"And when I finally left for my training in Gurgaon a week later, it was the last time I ever saw Sonali."

Chapter 23

The pitter-patter of the rain is the only sound in the drawing room for the longest time. Both Amit and Sunil have fallen silent. While one is lost in his memories, the other is trying hard to grapple with the pain he imagines the other must have gone through.

"Ahem . . ." Amit clears his throat. He wants to say something comforting to Sunil, but the extent of his loss staggers him and leaves him feeling hesitant and unsure of what to say. "I am sorry, Sunil," he says finally. "If I had any idea that your story is like this, I would have never pestered you to share it . . ."

Sunil nods his head, still a little lost in his memories of Sonali.

"So . . ." Amit hesitates, he wants to know what happened next, but he fears upsetting Sunil any further and almost does not want to hear what he knows will come next in the story.

"So," Sunil repeats, knowing that Amit wants him to continue with the story, but suddenly his strength has deserted him and he now wants to wrap the story up as soon as possible. "So, Sonali passed away while I was still in Gurgaon. I never got a chance to meet her again . . . to see her again . . ." Restless, Sunil gets up and walks to the balcony door. The rain drops trickle down the glass door in long lines. Sonali used to love the rain, he thinks to himself and smiles. With his back to Amit, he starts talking again, "Both me and Sonali bought Nokia cellphones before I left for Gurgaon, you know those old 1100 sets? We used to talk daily, at night, and sometimes during the day as well, if I had the time in between projects that is . . . much of our conversations were the same as before, but increasingly there was a hint of regret and longing in Sonali's words. It was almost as if she had figured out that her recovery was not what it should have been and that she was actually fast approaching death. There were days when she would be all excited and eager to know about my life in Gurgaon, when she'd make plans with me about what colour curtains to buy for our drawing room when we'd have a house of our own, and then, then there were days when she was trapped in a darkness of fear and regret, when she'd be sad and angry with her fate . . . she didn't want to die, she would keep saying . . . who does?" Sunil trails off, drawing long, deep breaths as if to steady himself. "Then one day, I called her in the morning before leaving for work, but she didn't pick up the phone. Thinking that she was either busy or not around, I didn't think too much of it. I called her again at night, but her phone was switched off. It struck me a little odd, she hadn't picked my call, she hadn't called back or texted even once during the entire day, and now her phone was switched off. The first niggling whispers of fear crept up then. But it was too late in the night for me to call up on her home landline and find out what was wrong. Sleep eluded me that night, and come morning, when the sky lightened up and the first rays of the sun broke through, I called up on Sonali's home landline. The minute I heard Uncle's phone, I knew it had happened. Sonali, I was told, had passed away the day before, on the thirteenth of November. I didn't ask for any details. I couldn't. Uncle couldn't speak either. I hurriedly disconnected the phone and felt my world crashing around me, falling into pieces, shattering, breaking, dissolving.

"The next couple of months were hard. I operated on automaton—eating, sleeping, bathing, working, doing only all those things which were necessary to keep myself alive. With Sonali gone, there was no reason for me to dream, to plan, to want anything. I dint care about living, I only existed.

"About two months after Sonali's death, I got a letter from Uncle. It was the most painful thing I have ever read . . . ah!" Sunil rubs his eyes, the memories overcrowding his mind, the wound feeling raw all over again.

Amit walks over to Sunil and hand him a refilled glass of water and pats him on the shoulder sympathetically. Sunil turns around to face him and smiles weakly. "Well," he says, "so that was the end of my story with Sonali . . ."

"Hmm . . . and Madhu? What about Madhu?" Amit asks.

"Yes, Madhu," Sunil nods, acknowledging that there is still a little bit of his story left. "I met Madhu again in 2009 at a training session in the Mumbai office of TCS. After Nine years had passed between our last meeting in Kalpi and this chance encounter in Mumbai . . . can you believe it? Nine long years . . ." Sunil shrugs, marvelling at the ways in which life works. "My world had turned upside down in these nine years . . . so much had happened, I had been through so much . . .

"After Sonali's death, I had immersed myself completely in work, working on project after project and not giving myself any time to think about Sonali or grieve too much. I went to USA for two years on a project and came home with enough savings to arrange Sharda's marriage, though finally, it was to my roommate and colleague Rajesh that she was married, and being a modern, educated man, he obviously did not ask for any dowry or anything like that. When after her marriage, my parents and the rest of my family began to pressurise me to get married, I wrangled yet another international project and left, managing to escape the pressure. But I couldn't stay away forever.

"I was forced to return to India in 2009 because the project I had been working on got scrapped. Soon after, I was sent for an advanced training session to Mumbai. And that's where I met Madhu.

"The first time I saw Madhu in the training hall, I didn't recognise her. I looked at her only as an attractive looking girl amongst all of us more-or-less similar-looking IT guys. But when she stared back at me, a flicker of recognition on her face, I wondered if I had seen her somewhere before. But it was only when she came up to me during the coffee break and said, "Sunil, is that really you?" that I recognised her. People change so much in nine years . . .

"We got talking then. As it turned out, we both were staying in the same guest house so we went back together after the day's session ended and had dinner together, talking all the while. The next four days went by in attending the training session during the day and in exchanging stories and bringing each other up to date about our lives after that. We also managed to explore a little bit of Mumbai. But I could not bring myself to tell Madhu about Sonali, the grief was too private, too deep for me to share it with her . . .

"We stayed in touch even after the training ended. She was posted in Bangalore and I was in Pune, but thanks to cellphones and the Internet, our friendship grew and blossomed once again and sometime in all those months, I finally told her everything there was to tell about Sonali and my love for her."

"Oh!" Amit interrupts. "How did she react to it?" he asks.

"She was very supportive to say the least, but for me, telling someone about everything and laying my feelings bare was like a release . . . I hadn't realised that all this time I had been walking around with an unbearably heavy weight on my heart. Once the words were all out there in the open between me and Madhu, I felt lighter . . . breathing became easier. Over the next couple of months, we both slowly fell in love with each all over again. It was harder for me, I struggled between my love for Sonali and my growing affection for Madhu. But I knew life was also all about moving on and letting the past be just that—your past. When Madhu suggested we meet in Mumbai for New Year's, I agreed quickly. And somehow on New Year's eve we found ourselves on the Juhu beach, watching the sun sink and give way to a beautiful starry night as the clock ticked it's into the New Year. Madhu must have known that the battle of emotions in my heart would prevent me from acknowledging the growing tenderness between us, and there, being the strong, sure-minded individual she has always been, she took it upon herself to broach the topic of our future together on that very night. Very gently did she broach the topic of getting married and settling down together. And by the end of it, just as the crowds around us started shouting and cheering through the countdown towards 2010, I turned to Madhu, and amidst all the people and all the noise and the fanfare, I leaned in and whispered into her ears, 'Yes, let's get married, Madhu!'

"10, 9, 8, 7, 6—

"'Yes!' Madhu whispered back, her eyes glistening with happy tears.

"5, 4, 3, 2—

"'I love you.'

"'I love you too.'

"1—

"'HAPPY NEW YEAR!'

Epilogue

Sunil reaches home early the next morning. The rain had not let off during the night and it had been difficult to drive back home, but he had started early, hardly having slept the night. All is quiet in his house when he lets himself in with his key.

He peeps into his bedroom and finds both Madhu, his wife, and his daughter, fast asleep in the master bedroom. His beautiful angels, the love of his life. He smiles, and gently closing the door behind him, he walks back to the kitchen where he quickly makes himself a strong cup of tea. Then, with the steaming cup of tea in his hand, he walks to his study and sits down at his desk. He is tired, but he knows he won't be able to sleep right away. His mind and his heart are too restless right now. Telling Amit about Sonali had awakened too many memories . . .

He takes a sip of the tea and relished the warmth of the hot beverage seeping into his body, then, keeping the cup on the desk, he bends down and opens the last drawer of the desk, and from underneath a stack of notebooks and diaries, he takes out a rather old and frayed looking envelope. Closing the drawer back with a gentle push, he keeps the envelope on the desk and stares at it. In neat writing, his name sits scrawled on the envelope. He draws a deep steadying breath and opens it, withdrawing a slightly old piece of folded paper. He stares at it for a long time, takes a sip of his tea, and then, he unfolds the paper and starts reading the words written on it . . . words written by a grieving father to his dead daughter's love.

20th January 2005,
Lucknow.

Dear Sunil,

It must be strange, to receive a letter from me like this . . . what do I say, beta, but I had a strong urge today to write to you.

How are you, Sunil? How is your work coming along? I hope you are putting in your best and working hard for those are the only two ways to success, but then again, I don't really need to say that to you, do I? I have always known you as a hardworking boy.

Beta, I wanted to thank you for everything. You went beyond the call of basic humanity to be there for Sonali, and for all of us. I cannot begin to tell you how thankful I have been for your presence in our lives through this time. You came into our lives as a young boy helping our Sanket become better in his studies, but you ended up becoming like a second son to both me and to Sonali's mother. And for Sonali, you were more than just a friend. I know, Sunil . . . I know how much Sonali loved you, and how much you loved her. And trust me, I would have been very happy to formalise your relationship and make you my son-in-law, but God had other plans for all of us . . .

Your parents are lucky indeed to have a son like you, they are truly blessed. I have seen how you put yourself below their needs and dreams. That is commendable and deserves great admiration and respect.

Sunil, I hope you understand why I did not tell you about Sonali's fading health. We both knew it was but a matter of time before she left us, but when you left for Gurgaon, I saw it as an opportunity for you to create a distance between yourself and Sonali which would enable you to bear the news of her death with a little more strength than you would have had you been here. I only had your best interest in mind . . . I could not bear to see you suffer through her death, not when you deserved a clean break, a chance to move on with your life and settle down.

I know the past month must have been difficult for you. Memories of Sonali have been haunting us every day. I keep thinking I can still hear the sound of her voice . . . but time, as they say, is the greatest healer of all . . . our wounds shall heal, Sunil and our hearts will mend and the pinch of this unbearable pain will fade little by little.

Sunil, I am not asking you to forget Sonali because I know that cannot happen. When we love someone, their memories are forever etched in our hearts, but both me and your Aunty want you to try and move on. Do well in your job, climb up the ladder, fulfil your dreams, and find someone to love. Life is meaningless if you do not have a partner to share it with . . . take it from me. It is difficult for me to say all this to you, if I could, maybe I would force you to stay bound to Sonali's memories for all of your life, but I cannot do that because I know you deserve a chance to live your life now. But more importantly, because I know that Sonali herself would have wanted you to move on . . . she said as much to her mother, asking her to make sure that you knew that she wanted you to move along in your life after she died. She had many many dreams, of living with you and creating a life together, but God had destined her journey to be a much shorter one than what we would have liked. Such are the way of the Almighty . . .

Beta, for all the times we have been selfish in asking too much of you, I do apologise. I am guilty of asking you to stay with Sonali even when I knew that there was no future for you with her . . . I still remember that day when I asked you to put your life on hold and be there for my daughter. That was selfish of me. I admit that, but I hope that you will someday forgive me and think of my selfishness as coming from my deep love for my daughter. I will always be obliged with your sacrifice of keep moving with Sonali in life even though knowing that there is no future in this relation.

We want only the very best for you now. May God always shower his choicest blessings on you. May you have a long fulfilling life ahead of you . . .

Yours
Sharma Uncle.

"Guess who?!"

A small child's voice squeals with delight even as tiny, plump hands close over Sunil's eyes.

"Oh! Who is it?!" Sunil exclaims, pretending to be surprised. He touches the hands covering his eyes. "Who is it? I can't see anything!" he exclaims playfully.

"Guess, guess, Papa!" the child says again.

"Hmm . . . let me see" Sunil says, making it sound as if he is actually thinking about who it could be. "Is it a fairy?"

"Nooooooo!" the little girl exclaims, thrilled that her father does not know who it is.

"I give up!" Sunil exclaims, pretending to surrender. "Just tell me who you are!"

"It is me, *Papa!* Sonaliiiiii!" the little girl removes her hands from Sunil's eyes and throws herself at him.

Sunil laughs and putting away the letter, he gathers her in his arms. Cuddling his daughter, feeling the warmth of that little body against his heart, he sends a silent prayer of heartfelt thanks to God above. Where life threw so many challenges at him once before, life has also been extremely generous to him in granting him his daughter. He turns his attention back to his daughter who has been saying something about her mother not wanting to wake up.

"Oh, is it?" he asks. "Mummy doesn't want to wake up is it?"

The little girl nods, excitement lighting up her lovely innocent eyes.

"Well then, let's go tickle her until she wakes up?"

"Yes!" his daughter exclaims, throwing her arms around his neck and hugging him with glee.

And with his daughter in his arms, Sunil walks out of his study to tickle his wife until she wakes up. It is going to be yet another day of simply joys and a whole lot of love in his world.

Acknowledgements

It was August 2010 and I was in Boston, US when, while on cruise, I got into an interesting discussion with a person, about the difficulty of identifying one's passion in life. He used the analogy of one's sweet tooth, which, while being extremely hard to pinpoint, was the single source of great pleasure. Ever since that day, I have been trying to find out my sweet tooth and now, having managed to write this book, I am beginning to strongly feel that writing is my sweet tooth, my passion. Thank you for helping me to reach this conclusion.

Thoughts are scattered and hard to keep a track of, but thoughts are what make a story, and I would, therefore, like to thank Anurag Aggarwal for motivating me and telling me to always pen down my thoughts. I had once dismissed his counsel, never thinking that mere thoughts had the potential to become a full-fledged story, but today, I am really grateful for his advice.

I would like to thank my father-in-law for mentoring me. Without his motivation and confidence, all of this would never have been possible. I would like to thank my mother and my mother-in-law as well, for without their lives as examples in front of me I would have never been the man that I am today. They are women who have dedicated their lives to their families.

Deepti, my wife, who has been both a shield against trouble and a constant source of inspiration and support, deserves the greatest thank-you of all. All my success is truly hers. I might get all the credit, but it is she who deserves the accolades.

A big thank you to all the organizations, where I am working/worked, for all the learning and thanks to my family & friends, Dr Manoj Kumar and Mr Jude Yep for all their support, prayers and wishes.

Thanks to Gauri, Sanjat, Pooja, Anurag, Arpan, Priyanka, Amit, Ankita, Suyash, Apoorva, Ankur, Umang, Prasi, Kartik and Pranay for proofreading the first draft of this book.

I would like to thank my sons Tanay and Tejas who always look at me as their role model. You motivate me to always do things better and lead a life which is more meaningful and worthy of you both.

And at last, A special thanks to my Editor who has done a fantastic job and my publisher.

Thank you

* * *